Sweet Farts #3
Blown Away

Other books by Raymond Bean

Sweet Farts #1

Sweet Farts #2: Rippin' It Old-School

Sweet Farts #3
Blown Away

RAYMOND BEAN

Visit www.raymondbean.com

amazon encore

Published by AmazonEncore
P.O. Box 400818
Las Vegas, NV 89140

ISBN-13: 978-1-612182-51-3
ISBN-10: 1-612182-51-8

Interior illustrations by Ben Gibson
Author photo by D. Weaver

For Stacy, Ethan, and Chloe.
Also, for Baba, who would do anything for us.

Contents

CHAPTER 1

I'm Keith Emerson, and I Just Farted!

I finished the last bite of my very first square apple and threw it into the woods.

"Wow, that was delicious," I shouted to Scott.

I was sitting in the dugout of the Sweet Farts, Incorporated, private baseball field. Scott was out at third base fielding balls from the new practice machine we created. We had taken a pitching machine and changed it around a bit so it shot ground balls, line drives, and pop-ups to the person in the field. It also turned to the left and the right so you never knew which way the ball was going to come at you. It was pretty awesome. Scott and I had sent the idea to the Yankees in hopes that they would order a few for their infield practice. They didn't.

"What?" Scott shouted as he dove for a line drive.

I walked out onto the field and shut off the machine. Scott was lying on the ground with infield dirt all over him.

"I said, those square apples are delicious. Have you had one yet?"

"Yeah, your grandma gave me one yesterday when I was working in my lab. They're awesome. I still can't understand why she gave that whole idea away."

"She didn't give it away; she's just donating the profits. She decided that the money her Square Fruit business was making was better spent on people who really needed it. She has it set up where the money goes to like five or six different charities."

"That's really nice and all, but she could have kept just a little, or I don't know," Scott smiled, "given it to me."

"That's my grandma. She's always thinking of everyone else. I think it's pretty cool. You know a lot of the money that Sweet Farts makes goes to charity, too?"

"Yeah, yeah," Scott said from the ground. "I know. You're a good boy, Keith. What I'd like to know is how I can become one of your charities. I could use a little more coin in *my* bank account."

"You kind of already *are* one of my charities."

"That hurts, Keith. That really hurts. You know, after my last experiment, I'm a little worried that Mr. Gonzalez is getting tired of me working at the lab."

Scott was right to be worried. His last experiment didn't exactly blow Mr. Gonzalez away. We were given several months to work on an idea for the fall science fair, but Scott had waited until the last minute. The morning of the fair, he had simply filled a two-liter soda bottle with colored water, and then taped another soda bottle to the top so the openings touched. It was the classic last-minute science fair project: tornado in a bottle.

"Here comes Mr. Gonzalez now. Let's ask him how he feels about you."

"Don't!"

Mr. Gonzalez was walking toward us. It was kind of funny seeing him out on the ball field in a suit. He usually stayed in the lab.

"Don't say a word," Scott said. "I don't think he's forgiven me for the tornado in a bottle." Scott rushed to his feet and wiped the dust from his clothes.

"Good afternoon, gentlemen," Mr. Gonzalez said. "I am very happy to see that you are both enjoying this wonderful day while the rest of us work in the lab. You two have to meet with Mr. Stuart in the development lab in about fifteen minutes. He needs to know what new Sweet Farts scents you will be putting out this summer. The tablets are selling well, but people are getting tired of the same old scents. We have too many obvious fruit and flower scents, like *Tangerine*, *Grape*, *Pickles*, and *Summer Rose*. Let's try to think up something more interesting."

My phone buzzed. It was another video message from Anthony. For his last science project he'd figured out a number pattern that allowed him to predict and win the lottery. His mom bought the winning ticket using the numbers he chose, and his family left for a trip around the world with all the money they had won. He had been sending me messages pretty much every day since they left. I shook my head and put my phone back in my pocket.

"Who was that?" Mr. Gonzalez asked.

"Let me guess," Scott said.

"Yep," I said, "that's why I didn't answer it."

"Who was it?" Mr. Gonzalez asked again.

"It's Anthony. He's been driving me nuts ever since he left on his trip."

"But he's been out of the country for months," Mr. Gonzalez said.

"He's been sending me messages from people he's met on his trip. They're basically teasing me in other languages. He's also doing ridiculous things and saying he's me. He sent a video the other day that I couldn't believe."

"What was he doing?" Scott asked.

"Don't ask me how he did it," I said, "but somehow he had a mask of my face made. The video showed him wearing the mask in what looked like some kind of fancy museum. There were people everywhere, and the place was dead quiet. He ripped one so loud that everyone around him turned and shot him The Look.

"At that moment he put his hands over his eyes and ran out shouting, 'I'm sorry I farted; my name is Keith Emerson.'"

Mr. Gonzalez chuckled a little. "I'll give it to the kid. He's creative."

Scott was amused, too, but didn't dare say anything with Mr. Gonzalez standing there.

"He's driving me crazy," I said. "I've been meaning to talk with you about him. I was hoping some time apart would help, but even with an ocean between us, he manages to pick on me constantly."

"Keith, we've talked about this before. Anthony has trouble showing people he cares about them in an appropriate way. It will get better over time."

"I don't think so, and I'm not interested in 'things getting better over time.' I want to kick him out of the company when he gets back from his trip."

"Really?" Scott asked. "I was just kidding when I said I wanted some of your money, Keith. Please don't fire me!" He put his hands together like he was praying.

"You're my best friend. I'm not going to fire you. I *do* want to fire Anthony, though," I said.

"I understand that Anthony is a handful, but he has a place in this company. He's very smart when he takes things seriously. Sometimes we learn the most from the people who challenge us. If I allowed myself to avoid every difficult personality I met, I would never have accomplished all of the things I have in my life. Besides, if you recall, you are the one who hired him in the first place," Mr. Gonzalez replied.

"I know, but that was a mistake. The only thing I'm learning from Anthony is how to be mean."

"Maybe you need to learn to stand up for yourself better," Mr. Gonzales suggested.

"I do stand up for myself," I insisted.

"Like I said, maybe you need to learn how to do it *better*. Now, I need you two sluggers to clean up and go meet Mr. Stuart about those new scents." He flashed me a smile and started to turn away.

"But, Mr. Gonzalez, I thought you put me in charge of Sweet Farts. If the company is mine, how come I can't fire Anthony?"

He turned back to face me again, "Sorry, Keith. I make the final decisions around here. Sweet Farts is your company, but it's part of my laboratory. I've said it before: in many ways, you guys are my own experiment."

CHAPTER 2

I Want Boogers

"We can't make farts smell like salami, Emma," I said, laughing. We had been at the development lab for a couple of hours, and we were getting a little crazy. We were supposed to have figured out what the new Sweet Farts scents were going to be days before. Mr. Stuart, the scientist assigned to help us, was not pleased. Grandma checked her watch for the second time and then searched her purse for her car keys.

Emma and Scott had the giggles. And when Emma gets the giggles, it makes everyone around her start laughing, too.

"Okay," she said, trying to catch her breath, "how about pastrami?" She struggled to hold back her laughter and look serious at the same time. "Or BOOGERS!"

This made me laugh harder than before, and Scott was cracking up so bad he seemed to have stopped breathing. After a big breath, he squeaked out, "Boogers don't have a smell."

"Okay, Emm," Grandma finally said, taking her keys from her purse. "I think that's enough work...and junk food for one day. We can talk about your interesting ideas on our way home. What do you say?"

"No way! More candy is the right thing, Grandma," Emma argued, again trying to sound serious.

"It's time to go, Sugar Pie. I think you've done enough for one day."

For most of the meeting, Emma had insisted on naming only lunchmeats as new scents for Sweet Farts. She'd suggested *Roast Beef* (but wanted to call it *Roast the Beast*), *Olive Loaf, Smoked Turkey, Pastrami, Salami,* and a bunch more. Basically, she named everything she could remember from the deli counter. At one point she suggested that one of the new scents should be *Ham.*

Scott's ideas were just as random and even more ridiculous. He came up with names like *Slap Shot, Grand Slam,* and *Three Pointer.* I kept explaining to him that those were sports terms and didn't have a smell. Neither of them seemed to get it. After Emma suggested *Boogers* as a scent, Scott had followed it up with *Field Goal.* I shook my head in disbelief and looked to my grandma for some help.

"I like them all," she said, giving me a smirk and jingling her keys playfully in Emma's direction. Grandma had a way of never getting worked up.

"Grandma, help me out here. We haven't come up with a single scent that is actually possible to use for Sweet Farts," I pleaded. I could feel Mr. Stuart glaring at me from across the table.

Emma stood up. "BOOGERS! BOOGERS! I INSIST ON BOOGERS!" She was out of her mind on sugar. She had eaten cotton candy and three donuts just since the beginning of the meeting. Mom and Dad were so happy that Emma was eating at all that they let her eat pretty much whatever she wanted, whenever she wanted it.

Emma's refusal to eat was the inspiration for my last science-fair project. Since then, though, she has been much better about eating all different kinds of foods, even some healthy ones.

Mr. Stuart finally lost his patience. "Keith, we've been in here half the day. You guys only need to come up with four scents. What are they going to be?"

I tapped my fingers nervously on the table. It was like everything else at the lab, all fun and games for the other kids, but I was the one who had to be mature.

"Keith?" Mr. Stuart asked again.

Grandma took Emma by the hand and headed for the door. Emma grabbed a fourth donut on the way out, but Grandma put it back. "We'll meet you in the car, boys," Grandma said, licking the icing off her thumb.

"We're going to have to get back to you, Mr. Stuart," I said, standing up. "I'll have the names of the new scents to you as soon as I can. Things are just a little crazy right now."

Scott looked at me and shifted uncomfortably in his seat. We had been given weeks to think of the new scents. With Anthony away, we'd had the place to ourselves. We didn't have a science project due for the first time since moving into the lab. Without a deadline, I'd finally been able to enjoy how fun the lab actually was. We played basketball and baseball, swam in the indoor pool, played video games, and just hung out. If we weren't in school, we were in the lab. It was paradise.

So why can't I think of four new scents and get it over with? I wondered. I guess I still needed a break from the work of Sweet Farts. The last science fair took more out of me than I thought. I had to admit that as much as I enjoyed doing science, it was nice to just be a regular kid again.

Mr. Stuart closed the folder in front of him. "If I don't have the new scents by the end of the week, I'm calling Mr. Gonzalez, and you guys can deal with him."

CHAPTER 3

No More School for the Guy in the Dress

The party officially ended the next day. I'd known it was only a matter of time until Anthony returned.

"I'm baaaack," he announced, marching onto the basketball court at the lab, wearing what I can only describe as a dress. It was about noon, and Scott and I were shooting baskets. "My trip around the world is complete. My genius mind returns to you." He turned to me. "I know you missed me, Lord of the Farts. I hope you didn't cry too much," he said as he held up his hand for a high five. I halfheartedly tried to return it, but he moved his hand out of the way just in time. I shook my head. I should have known better.

"Scott, I hope you weren't too bored having to spend your time with the Goozer here." Anthony had that obnoxious smirk on his face that I've grown to really dislike over the years.

"It's good to see you, too, Anthony," I said.

"What was your trip like?" Scott asked.

"Completely awesome, thank you for asking. And now that I have returned, I think I should let you guys know right away that I'm not going to school anymore."

I didn't want to hear whatever nonsense Anthony was talking about. I checked the time. We only had a few more minutes until the Sweet Farts meeting started, and I was excited to show off my new meeting room.

"I'm sure it's a fascinating story, but we don't have time to get into it right now. Our meeting is about to start," I said.

"Well, welcome home, and might I say that's a beautiful dress you are wearing, Miss Papas," Scott said.

"It's a sarong. And you would know that if you had ever traveled farther than the mall before. They're very popular in Thailand."

"Well, you look pretty in it," I said and bowed. It was rare that I actually got the upper hand on Anthony when trading insults.

"Wow, Keith, that was actually pretty funny. How unlike you. Still, this happens to be the most comfortable thing I've ever worn. And, dress or no dress, you two geniuses will still have to go to elementary school tomorrow, and the guy in the 'dress' will never go to school again."

"What do you mean?" Scott asked. "You have to go to school. You're a kid."

"We don't have time for this right now," I reminded them.

Anthony held his hand to his chin like he was thinking. "I might as well just come out and say it. I am going to be home schooled." He clapped his hands three times loudly and yelled, "ENTER!" A woman, who must have been waiting outside the door, walked in and flashed us a fake smile. She seemed very professional and looked dressed for business. In her hands, she held two large bags full of books. "Meet my tutor, Mrs. Weaver."

"Okay, Anthony," she said, "I let you do that once to show off for your friends, but don't expect me to agree to that 'enter' thing again. I'm going to start setting up. Which way is your lab?"

Anthony pointed down the hall. "Last door on the left; just follow the smell of chlorine from my private pool."

"Wonderful," she said mockingly. "Are you going to introduce me to your friends?"

"Of course," Anthony said cunningly. Then he added, "*Ciò è la macchina che del fart gli ho detto circa,*" and they both started laughing.

"What did he say?" I asked.

"Nothing important. You must be Keith. I'll be working with Anthony, but if you guys need any help with your schoolwork, let me know." She shook my hand and said hello to Scott. Then she hauled her bags down the hall toward Anthony's lab.

When she was gone, Anthony added, "Did I say home schooled? Let me rephrase that. I am going to be 'lab' schooled. I will spend my days here at Sweet Farts, Inc., swimming in the pool, practicing my swing, shooting baskets, and enjoying the luxuries a young genius like me requires, while you two kids attend elementary school."

"You wish," I said. It wasn't the best comeback, but I was a little rusty.

"Actually, I did *wish*, Keith, but now that wish has become a reality."

"You don't think Mr. Michaels and Mr. Cherub at school will have a problem with you skipping out every day?" Scott asked.

"They have no say. My mom signed the papers, Mrs. Weaver is paid in full, and Mr. Gonzalez has already agreed to it. You kids better get right home after the meeting tonight. You're going to need all your rest for school tomorrow. I'm planning on sleeping in." He grabbed the basketball from my arms and dribbled down the court. He tried to dribble through his legs, but the ball got caught on the bottom of his sarong. He stumbled, scooped the ball up, and launched it toward the basket, even though he was way too far away to make the shot.

Yep, the party is officially over, I thought.

CHAPTER 4

Uprising

Twenty minutes later, everyone was finally gathered in the boardroom. Scott, Emma, Grandma, and Anthony were all sitting around the awesome new table I'd had delivered the day before. I was so excited that it had come in time for the meeting. The table was shaped like a baseball: round and white with the red stitching and everything, and all the chairs were made of soft leather and shaped like baseball mitts, monogrammed with the employee's name and then *Sweet Farts, Inc.* stitched underneath.

"Okay," I began, standing up. "I wanted to bring you all together to talk about the future of the company and set some new goals. I think you would all agree that Sweet Farts, Inc., has accomplished a lot in a short time. So, I thought it would be a good idea to go around the room and take a minute to talk about the projects each of you is currently working on."

"I love the new table, Keith," Grandma said.

"Yeah, and these chairs are awesome," Emma added, spinning hers in a circle. When Anthony stood, I foolishly thought he was about to compliment me.

"Before we get started, Mr. Farts, I have something to announce."

"Anthony, you spent all that time traveling the world and you still feel the need to call me Farts? That hasn't grown old to you yet?" Anthony had been calling me names for years. In fourth grade, he nicknamed me Silent But Deadly, and I've been known as S.B.D. ever since. Then last fall, Anthony and Scott found a Web site that translated words into other languages. Some of their favorite international nicknames for me were *Prut*, *Goozer*, and *Winderigheid*, all words for passing gas.

"Oh no, it's still as fun as the first time, Senior Farts. But that's not what I want to discuss." He leaned back in his mitt and linked his hands together across his chest. "Before we go any further,

I think we should have a vote to decide who should be in charge of this company."

"Anthony! I started the company, and I'm the one Mr. Gonzalez put in charge. So, the answer to that question is ME. Now, moving on..."

He interrupted. "Well, I gave it a lot of thought on my trip, and I have come to the conclusion that this company needs new leadership. I mean, you didn't even come up with an idea that worked for the last science fair! You tried to turn candy canes into liver sticks or whatever, and in the end you had nothing but a terrible-tasting idea."

"Yeah, maybe, but science isn't about being right all the time. It's about experimenting. Besides, that idea is still in development. While you were roaming around the world, I was back here in the lab working on it. I think I'm pretty close to perfecting Liver Canes."

"Yeah, you said you were pretty close before I left, too. In case you don't remember, I was off roaming the world because I beat a little thing called the LOTTERY."

"We all know what you did for the last fair, Anthony."

"Hey!" Emma called out in mid spin. "Why are you guys arguing? You both did a great job. Keith gave me a new candy cane to try just yesterday, Anthony."

"How was it, Emm?" I asked.

She stopped spinning. "Oh, well, it was terrible, but I know you will do it someday," she said, giving me two thumbs up.

"Well, I say that my experiment makes me the smartest guy in the company, which also means that I should be in charge."

"You are definitely not the smartest guy in this company. *MY* company. So, what you should be saying is 'Thanks for the opportunity to work here, Keith.'"

"No, that's not what I'm trying to say at all, Toots. I came up with my number-pattern hypothesis on my own. I built my extension to the lab with my own money. So, I think what *you* are trying to say is, 'Thanks for keeping my lame company going because my last experiment stunk.'"

"If you don't like working here so much, why don't you start your own company?"

"I would love to, but Mr. Gonzalez made me and my mom sign a contract before I built the indoor pool and extra space in the lab. It says that I can't start a company of my own. We agreed that I would stay a part of this stink bomb company of yours until I'm eighteen."

I almost choked. The thought of working with Anthony until I was eighteen was a nightmare!

"What I did not agree to was just sitting back and allowing you to run this company into the ground."

I looked at Scott for a little support, but he was playing his video game and listening to music in his earphones. He looked at me, made a rock-star face, and sang something in a low whisper that sounded like, "You ain't gonna take a bobidy baah baah, yeah." Shaking my head, I turned my attention to Emma, my newest employee. She was petting a baby bunny. Her new dog, Goofy, was sprawled out on the floor next to her.

"You boys need to learn to get along. I don't know why you have to argue," she said. "I like being at the lab. It's so much fun."

"Fun? This is exactly what I mean, Keith. You hired your little sister to work in the lab? What do you expect her to accomplish here anyway? As far as I can see, all she has done is fill this place up with animals."

Anthony was sort of right. Since Emma had started working at the lab, she hadn't done much more than buy baby animals and play with them.

"I like my animals. They are so cute and they make me happy." She hugged her bunny. "His name is Mr. Cuddlesworth."

Anthony said, "Good grief!" and fell back into his chair.

"If you ask me, boys, Emma's got the right idea," Grandma added. "She is enjoying herself. Can you two say the same?" Grandma gave Emma a fist bump, and then they both opened their hands to "blow it up."

This was crazy. Why was no one defending me?

Anthony swiveled toward me. "Keith, I've had it with the way you 'run' this company. I am going to figure out a way to take it over."

"Since you made your *amazing* lottery discovery, you haven't even been here. I'm the one who's been running the lab and making this place more awesome. I'm the one who ordered that super cool baseball mitt chair you're sitting in right now."

Anthony looked at me, shrugged, and ripped one into the seat. "That's what I think of your chair. Maybe you can be the decorator and leave the important stuff to me. I'm going to end up being the one who runs this company, Farts. You know it; I know it; even Mr. Cuddlesworth knows it."

CHAPTER 5

A Gabilliony Dollars

Mom picked Grandma, Emma, and me up after the meeting was over. I couldn't believe Scott played his video game the whole time and Emma just sat there petting Mr. Cuddlesworth. Worse still was Anthony farting in the new chair I'd ordered him. The guy had no respect. Having him around again reminded me that we'd had a pretty fart-free environment the past few months. Even Emma had outgrown her farting stage since she'd started working at the lab. From the back seat I asked, "Mom, what do you think about giving me permission to get a home tutor? I could get my schoolwork done at the lab, and you wouldn't have to keep driving me back and forth between the lab and school."

She looked at me in the rearview mirror. "Come on, Keith, you can't be serious. Do you really think I'm going to allow you to spend the whole day at that lab playing with your friends?" It was dark, so I wasn't able to see her face to tell how against my idea she was.

"Mom, I'm not going to be playing. Sweet Farts is a multimillion-dollar company. I think it would be good for me to spend more time there and less time at school. You can even pick the tutor."

"I'll be your tutor," Grandma offered.

"I don't want to go to school, either," Emma announced. "Now that I'm working in the lab I get *whatevow* Keith gets, right, Mommy? And I want to spend all day with *Gwandma*."

"No, you don't, Emma," I said. "And why are you talking like a baby all of a sudden? At the lab you were pronouncing your words perfectly. How come when you're around Mom you talk like a baby?"

"Keith, leave your sister alone. Don't take it out on her just because you aren't getting what you want." She shot Grandma a look. "And you're not helping here."

We pulled into the driveway, and I couldn't help but think how great it would be if we bought another house someday. Ours was nice, don't get me wrong, but it was small for the four of us.

"Mom, why don't you let me spend a little of that Sweet Farts money on a new house already? It's kind of silly that we have millions of dollars in the bank, and we're still living in the same house."

"This house is our home," Mom said. "There is no reason for us to buy a bigger one. The money your company makes from the sale of Sweet Farts is for your future. We've talked about this a million times."

We all got out of the car, hugging and high-fiving Grandma before she drove away in her VW Bug, her music thumping as she rolled down the street.

I tried again, "I know the money is for my future, but how nice would it be to have a pool and a little more room?"

"It would be very nice, and if we decide to do something like that, your father and I will be the ones paying for it, not our ten-year-old son."

"How about if I make a GABILLIONY DOLLARS? Will you let me buy you a *bigga* house then?" Emma asked in her cutest voice, as Mom opened the front door. I didn't say anything about the fact that Emma said "bigga" and not *bigger.* Mom didn't seem to want to accept the fact that Emma could talk just fine. She used the cute, "mispronounce her words thing" to get what she wanted and seem ultra-cute. And it usually worked.

"Aww, Emma, when you make a GABILLIONY DOLLARS, you can buy us all a bigger house," Mom said.

Dad was standing just inside the door when we walked in, and he joined right into the conversation. "Awesome! Are we finally going to get a new house with all that sweet Sweet Farts money?" he asked.

Mom handed him the grocery bags in her arms. "No, honey, we agreed not to allow our millionaire son to buy us a new house, remember?"

"I'm going to buy us a new house when I make a GABILLIONY DOLLARS!" Emma announced skipping down the hall toward her room.

"Dad, what do you think about me getting a homeschool tutor and doing all my schoolwork at the lab?" I asked, as we walked toward the kitchen.

"Oh man, that was my dream when I was a kid," he said, putting the groceries down on the counter. "No school so I could stay at home all day and sleep in. That would have been the BEST! And you've got the pool and the basketball court right there..." He caught Mom's eye and realized he was on the wrong side of this argument. "I mean to say, those were my *childish* dreams, son. Having a homeschool tutor would be a terrible idea for *you*. *You* should be going to school." He glanced again at Mom with a big cheesy smile and then looked back at me and shrugged.

Mom said, "Let's get dinner ready and then it's off to bed. Like it or not, you have school tomorrow, Mr. Moneybags."

CHAPTER 6

Good Morning, Big Boy

The next morning my phone started buzzing at seven o'clock. I rolled over and tried to ignore it. But it kept buzzing so I finally answered it. "Rise and shine, Sweet Cheeks. The school bus will be there in about an hour for you." I hung up before Anthony could get anything else out. *Unbelievable,* I thought.

It started ringing again, but this time it was Scott, thankfully. "I'm so jealous of Anthony! How are we going to get in on that home schooling gig?"

"I don't know, my mom won't even think about it. What about your mom?"

"No way, she doesn't even like me going to the lab as much as I do right now. She said that last year I spent all my time there, and all I had to show for it was a tornado in a bottle."

"Well she's sort a right, isn't she?"

"Yeah, but I was young then. I'm much more mature now."

"Right," I said. "I'll see you on the bus."

After I hung up, I noticed that I had a few new e-mails. I opened the first one, and it was a picture of Anthony sitting at my new baseball table having a huge breakfast. The second e-mail was a picture of him doing a cannonball into his awesome indoor pool (which meant his tutor took the picture, which was just ridiculous), and the third e-mail had a video of Anthony. He was standing on home plate on *my* baseball field and singing, "Take me out to the ball game, take me out to the crowd. I'm getting home schooled and you are not. Enjoy your gross lunch and also this…" (And then he held the microphone to his rear end and ripped one.)

I need to change my e-mail, I thought.

CHAPTER 7
The Kilt

After school I met with Mr. Gonzalez in his office at the lab.

"Why didn't you tell me that you made Anthony agree to work at Sweet Farts, Inc., for the rest of his life?" I asked.

"Eighteen is hardly 'the rest of his life,' but I did that to make sure that you all continue to work together. His mother agreed. We felt it would provide you two with focus and help you stick to a common goal. So I'm afraid you're stuck with each other for now."

"But, Mr. Gonzalez, he's mean to me, he's rude, and he farts all the time. Is he really someone we want working for the company?"

"Keith, Anthony's proven that he's a smart kid. He showed the most potential during the last science fair, and I like that he challenges you. Just because you two are butting heads right now doesn't mean you should stop working together. Some of the people I've learned the most from in my life have been the hardest to deal with. If I'd avoided everyone who challenged me or made things hard on me, I would have never become as successful as I am today. In fact, let's call Anthony and Scott in here so we can talk about a few things." He clicked the intercom on his desk. "Anthony and Scott, please come to my office right away."

I couldn't believe Mr. Gonzalez was so set on keeping Anthony around. He thought Anthony *challenged* me, but he was a *bully* to me.

Anthony walked in a few minutes later wearing a T-shirt and a checkered skirt that stopped at his knees.

"What did I tell you, Mr. Gonzalez? He can't even dress normal," I said.

"I'm wearing a kilt. I got it in Scotland when I visited a few months ago. What do you have against Scotland?" he asked, as he sat down next to me.

"I don't have anything against Scotland. It's just that you aren't from Scotland, and this is the second time this week you've worn a dress."

Just then, Scott walked in, and he was wearing a kilt, too. He looked at me and curtsied.

"You, too?" I asked. "Are you guys working on next year's Halloween costumes?"

"It was a gift from Anthony. It may look strange, but I kind of like it. You should give it a try. Besides, they're from *Scot*-land. How awesome is that? Get it, *Scott*-land? I think I'd like it there." He spun in a circle to really give me the whole picture. "Where's yours?"

"I didn't get one for the Fartmaster here because I knew he would be too narrow-minded to appreciate it," Anthony said without looking at me.

"All right, enough, you guys," Mr. Gonzalez said. "This constant fighting and picking on each other isn't doing anyone any good."

Anthony nodded. "That's an interesting point, Mr. G. I was just saying to Keith at our last meeting that we need some new leadership. I had myself in mind."

"You guys need to start thinking like a team and working together, Anthony," Mr. Gonzalez replied.

"Yeah, Anthony, you heard him; we're a team so it would be nice if you gave me a break on all the teasing." *Not bad*, I thought. *I stood up to him pretty well, and in front of Mr. Gonzalez to boot.*

Anthony rolled his eyes. "You were the one making fun of my kilt a few minutes ago, Fart Art. Don't dish it out if you can't take it. But you should know that I can take it all day long."

"Whatever," I managed.

"Well, don't get too comfy," Mr. Gonzalez warned. "I called you guys together to let you know that I've entered you in the All-World Science Challenge, taking place in New York City in a few months. This time around you won't just be competing against other kids from your school. Your work will be judged against the work of young scientists from around the world. Also, only one idea from this lab will be presented at the AWSC."

My heart sank. This was the exact opposite of what I needed.

"Whose idea will be entered in the challenge?" Anthony asked.

"Your guess is as good as mine," Mr. Gonzalez said with a smile. "You will all work on a project of your own during the months leading up to the competition. As always, you will have help from the scientists at my lab if you need it. And the week before the AWSC, you will decide as a group which project will represent Sweet Farts, Inc., at the challenge."

"What's the prize?" Scott asked eagerly.

"The prize is not the important thing here, Scott. The important thing is the process. You guys have a few interesting discoveries under your belts. Now you'll be exposed to what some other young scientists around the world are working on."

I tried again. "I don't know, Mr. Gonzalez; we might just need a little time off. The last science fair was only a few months ago, and I'm still working on my molecular gastronomy project…"

"Keith, I didn't set this lab up so that you could work on your baseball swing, practice your basketball shots, and play video games. This is a *lab*, and you are all expected to work on science if you are going to continue to utilize this space. Now, I suggest you guys head back to your labs, stop arguing with each other, and get to work."

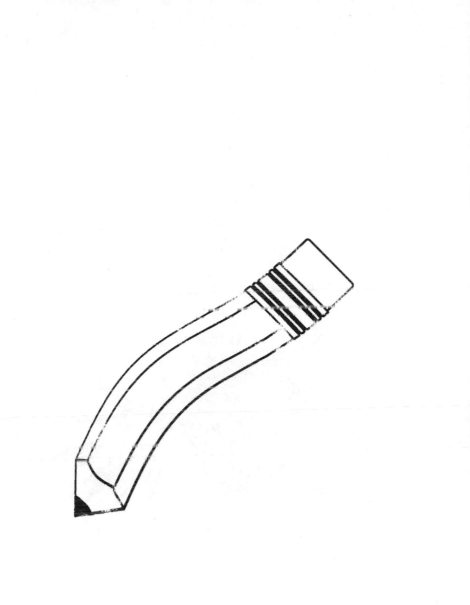

CHAPTER 8

Roland the Farter

I was really annoyed, and not because I have a problem working on science projects. It was because I knew how much drama this whole challenge was going to create with Anthony. I knew he was going to get all crazy about this new competition and drive me nuts.

"So, Anthony, what did you do all that time you were traveling, anyway? You were gone for a long time," Scott asked, as the three of us walked out onto the basketball court and started taking shots.

"Remember when you and I were on the computer looking up how to say *fart* in other languages?" Anthony asked.

"Well, *I* do. You guys would turn whatever word you thought was funny into a new nickname for me," I reminded him.

"That's right, Gooz, excellent memory. Well, doing all that research got me interested in different cultures."

I couldn't believe Anthony was saying that his desire to travel the world came from looking up the word *fart* in different languages.

"I couldn't help but wonder about all the other things I didn't know about the rest of the world. I figured if I thought that one word was interesting, there must be other amazing things about those cultures, too."

"Like what?" I asked. "How to say *burp* and *doo-doo*?"

"Well, if you must know, Mr. Negative, I found out a lot of things about myself on this trip. It turns out that I have ancient roots." A real seriousness seemed to come over him. Then he grinned. "Have you guys ever heard of Roland the Farter?"

CHAPTER 9
IQ Test

"Roland the Farter was a minstrel in the court of Henry the Second of England. I learned about him on my trip. Legend has it that every year on Christmas day, Roland was expected to perform for the king and his guests. The highlight of his performance was a jump, a whistle, and a fart. He was able to do them all at once and on command! Can you guys imagine it?" Anthony had a look of amazement on his face.

"So what does that weirdo have to do with you and your trip? You said you 'found yourself'?" I asked. I couldn't tell if Anthony was really nuts or if he was just messing with us. Even Scott was looking at him strangely.

"I did. And Roland was not a weirdo, and neither am I. When I learned about Roland the

Farter, I really connected to his story. You see, he was a flatulist just like me."

"What's that?" Scott asked.

Anthony ripped a stinker.

"Come on," Scott pleaded. "That's not right."

Continuing as if nothing had happened, Anthony said, "A flatulist is someone who can fart on command." He did it again to make his point. "I always knew I could do it. How do you think I was able to torture you so well at school, Keith?" he asked as he slapped me on the back. "I just never knew the name for it. Now I do. My name is Anthony Papas, and I'm a flatulist!" he shouted.

"So, you admit it was *you* farting all those times at school?" I said, victoriously. To this day, Anthony still hadn't come clean to anyone else at school about his gas.

"Not to anyone other than you guys. To everyone else, I'll forever blame my gas on you, Keith. Of course, if you step down as the head of Sweet Farts, I might consider *not* blaming you for my farts anymore."

"You might be the most stubborn person I've ever known," I said. "You just don't know when to quit. How in the world did I ever end up hiring you for this company?"

"I think you know the answer to that question. I am the smartest guy you know. In fact, I think we should make a little bet on who is smarter: you or me."

I was dribbling, and Anthony was now guarding me, trying to steal the ball.

Emma walked in from outside. A baby goat was following her, and Goofy, her dog, was right at her side. "Let me guess, you two are fighting again," she said.

"Okay, Anthony, what kind of wager do you want to put on it?" I asked, dribbling to my left. I knew this was a bad idea. Anthony had a way of tricking me and making me look foolish. But there was no way he was smarter than I was.

"How about your company? We both take an IQ test, and the one with the highest IQ is in charge of the company," Anthony said, swiping at the ball.

"What's an IQ?" Emma asked from the sidelines.

"It's a test that you take to see how smart you are," Anthony answered.

"Well, if we're taking a smarts test to see who is running Sweet Farts, then I want in on it, too," Scott said, making a face as his shot missed the hoop.

I stopped dribbling and held the ball tight. "We aren't going to take an IQ test to find out who the smartest person in the company is," I said.

"No, we're going to take an IQ test to see who should be *running* the company," Anthony said, smiling.

I glanced around and all three of them were staring at me. Even the goat was looking at me. Anthony was doing the same thing he had been doing to me at school for almost two years— pressuring me into situations for his benefit. Only, now he was doing it in my own company.

"Mr. Gonzalez put me in charge of this company. So if you guys want to take an IQ test to see who should be running things, he's the man to talk to, not me." I wasn't sure how Anthony turned this into a way to try and snake away my company, but I hoped telling him to talk with Mr. Gonzalez would end it.

"So you admit that I'm smarter than you?" Anthony asked, not letting up.

"No, I didn't say that. I just said that I'm not able to make this kind of decision. We should talk to Mr. Gonzalez."

"Keith, he put you in charge. But he also said we had to work together. If you're so smart, why don't you accept my challenge?"

"I just think it's silly." I didn't really think Anthony was smarter than me, but he was very tricky. Maybe he would come out smarter on an IQ test. I didn't even know anything about IQ tests. For all I knew, he'd been traveling around studying for one the past few months. He did have a personal tutor now.

"Well, I think Keith is the smartest guy in the company," Emma chimed in.

Finally, someone on my side, I thought.

"Why? Because he's your brother?" Scott asked.

"No, because he's the only boy on the court actually dressed for basketball."

CHAPTER 10

Emma's Lab

Later on that day, I walked out back knowing I'd find Emma and Grandma there. Emma was sitting on the ground in front of a small barn feeding the baby goat a bottle.

Her friends, John and Ruby, were on the ground with her, laughing up a storm and playing with Goofy.

In the months since I hired Emma, she had planned her outdoor lab with the help of Mom, Grandma, and Mr. Gonzalez. She didn't want a space inside the lab with the rest of us. Her area was outside. It was basically a mini-farm. There were a bunch of fenced-in areas and small barns. It was a five-year-old's dream come true.

After the space was set up, the first animal Emma got was a puppy. She always wanted a puppy, but our house was too small. I was pretty psyched, too, even though I would have gotten something like a golden retriever, or one of those Frisbee dogs. She chose a rescue dog, which meant it was at the pound, and Emma gave it a home. I liked the fact that she saved the dog from the pound, but we didn't even know what kind of dog it was. It was brown, black, white, tan, gray, you name it! The dog was just funny looking so Emma named her Goofy.

After saving Goofy, Emma quickly moved on to bunnies, goats, and any other furry little animal she could think of. I told Mr. Gonzalez I didn't think it was a good idea for a girl as young as her to be in charge of all those baby animals, but he told me they were part of her scientific work. As far as I could tell, Emma's scientific work was mostly just play dates with her friends. Still, I figured I had my baseball field and my basketball court; if Emma wanted to clean up animal poop all day that was her choice.

"Hi, Keith," Emma said with a huge smile on her face. Her friend John got up and shook my hand.

"Hi, Keith, *pleasha* to meet you, I'm Jonathan Cuzzie," he said. I thought it was pretty funny that a five-year-old was being so formal.

"It's nice to meet you, too, Jonathan," I said. "You're a polite little guy."

"Thank you, Mr. Farts. Can I work here?"

"First of all, Jonathan, please don't call me Mr. Farts. Second of all, no, you can't work here because you're too young."

Jonathan's lip started to tremble. "I didn't mean to call you Farts. Emma said it was your name."

I looked at Grandma, who was sitting on a nearby bench. She shrugged. "Why can't Emma hire a few of her friends to work at the lab? You hired Anthony and Scott," she said.

"Yeah, I want to hire two friends, too," Emma said, handing Jonathan a fluffy white bunny. "Here, Jonathan, can you keep an eye on this little guy while I talk with Keith?" Jonathan nodded and walked back toward the other bunnies.

"I don't think so, Emma. I think it's fine if you want to have your friends here for play dates, or whatever you want to call it, but you can't have your own employees."

"Fair is fair," Grandma said. "I don't see why Emma can't form her own little science team."

This whole place is getting crazier by the minute, I thought. Anthony and Scott were walking around in kilts, and now my baby sister wanted to hire employees.

"Grandma, she isn't even doing science back here. She's just playing with baby animals."

"I love my babies. They're so cute. I just can't take it!" She leaned down and gave Goofy a big squeeze and looked up at me with her big eyes. Ruby had taken over feeding the goat the rest of the bottle, and there were baby bunnies everywhere. There were at least seven of them. I didn't even know where they'd all come from. Emma scooped up a black one with white spots and big floppy ears.

I had to admit the whole scene was pretty cute. But Sweet Farts wasn't in the cute business. We were in the science business.

"Want to hold the cute little bunny, Keith?" she asked.

"No thanks, Emm. I just wanted to get away from Anthony for a little while. He's making me crazy. It was much calmer around here when he was away."

She smiled at me. "Play with bunnies! Playing with bunnies always makes me happy. Why do you think I'm out here all the time?" She said this as if it were the most obvious thing in the world.

John and Ruby both insisted I play with bunnies, too. Then they all started chanting, "Play with the bunnies, play with the bunnies."

Grandma smiled from the bench. "Play with the bunnies," she said, joining in the chant.

"I just needed to get away from Anthony for a while. I'm not out here to play with bunnies."

"What's wrong with bunnies?" Emma asked.

"Nothing, Emm, it's just that I'm a guy, and guys aren't into all that cutesy stuff."

"I'm a guy, and I think bunnies ROCK!" John shouted, pumping his fist in the air.

"It's okay if you want to hold the bunny, Keith," Grandma teased.

"I'll see you guys later. I need to get back to my lab and figure out what I'm going to do for this crazy science challenge."

"Okay, good luck," Emma said. She turned around and headed back to the bunnies.

"Wait, what are you going to do? You're part of the company now, you know," I reminded her.

"I don't want to be in a contest. I just want to take care of my beautiful babies," she called without turning back.

I looked at Grandma. "She can't just hang out back here and play with baby animals all day. She has to do some science."

"She'll be just fine, Keith. I'm working with her. You just worry about yourself."

Grandma was right. I needed to focus. Walking back to the lab, I could hear Emma and her friends chanting, "Play with the bunnies, play with the bunnies."

CHAPTER 11

Liver Canes

I had to figure out something amazing to enter in the All-World Science Challenge. For the past few months, I had been *kind of* working on the molecular gastronomy project I'd started for the last school science fair. My objective was to create a liver cane—a candy cane that had all the vitamins and healthy stuff in liver (which is gross) with the great taste of a candy cane. Emma hadn't been eating at the time I thought of the experiment, so it had seemed like a great way to help her and other kids who don't like to eat healthy foods.

I mean, wouldn't it be great if your cauliflower tasted like chocolate? Or, if every gross healthy food tasted like ice cream? The work had to be done. Mr. Stuart and some of his assistants were helping me out with the real difficult science of the experiment. I think they were all getting a little tired of eating liver, too.

The problem was, I was stuck. The only way I could think of to make the liver taste like candy canes was to add sugar to it. And that was not a solution to the problem, so I had been working hard, trying to understand the molecular structure of the food and how I could change it in some way. It felt hopeless, but I kept on trying. I can't even begin to tell you how much liver I had eaten over the past few months. Looking back, I probably should have experimented with something a little tastier until I got the science right. It would definitely take a lot more work to get the liver canes perfected enough to enter them in the AWSC.

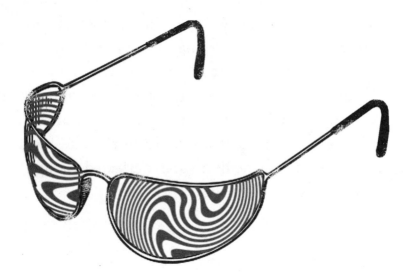

CHAPTER 12

Scott-tacular!

I decided to take a break and head over to Scott's lab, which I was surprised to see had changed a lot since the last time I was in it. One section of the room was an exact replica of his bedroom. It had a bed that looked just like his, the same posters on the wall, and even a messy desk. It was weird seeing his entire room in the lab.

"What are you working on?" I asked. "I hope this isn't all so you can nap here."

"Very funny, Keith. Actually, I'm working on a little thing I like to think of as the greatest discovery since, well, Sweet Farts."

"Okay, what'ya got?" I asked. Scott was dressed in a white lab coat, and there were several scientists bustling around the lab working on different experiments. I was impressed.

"Okay, so you know how you and I have really small houses?"

"Yeah, I've noticed that my house is small."

"Well, I am working on Virtual Reality Housing." As he said it, he held his hands up in front of him like he was picturing a billboard of some sort.

"What are you talking about?"

"I am talking about an invention so amazing that it will change the way you live. I am trying to create special glasses that when you put them on, like so," he paused, putting on a pair of very dark glasses, "they change your boring, old, ordinary house into a sweet mansion. Sweet Mansion Keith, can you picture it?"

"I'm not sure I follow. How can glasses change the look of your house?"

"These glasses would create a virtual world inside your house. For example, let's say you had a bed in your house, like the one you have now. You know, a lame bed. With these glasses, you could get rid of it and replace it with a virtual bed."

"Hey, I like my bed," I protested.

"Well, just imagine if in place of your bed, with the help of the Virtual Reality Scott-Thousands, it would look like one of those fancy beds they have at hotels. And if you lived in small house with no furniture at all, you could set the whole place up with virtual reality furniture. The room would be completely empty, but when you put on the glasses, you would be able to set it up however you wanted. I'm talking a virtual couch, desk, TV, you name it."

"Did you just say, 'Scott-Thousand'?"

"Yes, but that's not the important part of this story. The important thing is that people in small houses, who don't have a lot of money, will be able to buy these amazing glasses and change their boring, old houses into a Scott-tacular home."

"Why do you keep adding your name to every word?"

"Because, Keith, I have finally found it. This is my Sweet Farts, my lottery! This is the discovery that is going to be Scott-tacular!"

"I like your idea. I just don't know how practical it is. I mean, even if you can create glasses that would change the look of my house and let me see furniture that isn't really there, what happens when I go to sit on my virtual reality bed?

Wouldn't I just fall on the floor? It sounds a little far-fetched."

"So did a little invention called Sweet Farts. If you remember, I thought you were crazy when you set out to find the cure for the common fart back in fourth grade. Now it's time for my amazing idea. I need your support, though. You have to believe in the Scott-tacular ideas I'm cooking up for your company."

What Scott was talking about seemed like science fiction, but he had a point. Sweet Farts sounded like a pretty crazy idea at one time, and it had become a reality. "Okay, Scott. You're right. A lot of people thought I was nuts with the Sweet Farts idea, until I proved them wrong. So go ahead. Keep working on your idea. Prove *me* wrong."

"You don't think I can do it, do you?" Scott asked.

"Not even a little bit, but I like that you're trying. It beats a tornado in a bottle any day. I think it's Scott-tacular!"

CHAPTER 13

Singing Insult-o-gram

The next morning was like every other that week. Anthony woke me with e-mails and phone calls. There were the usual videos of him doing things to make me jealous, like swimming, shooting baskets, and playing video games. It was getting a little old.

Lying in bed in that half-asleep, half-awake stage, I could hear Emma and Mom downstairs and could smell coffee and bacon. I knew it was time to wake up, but I just didn't want to get out of bed. The rain was splashing against my bedroom window and beating on the roof. Then I heard a loud KNOCK, KNOCK, KNOCK from downstairs. I sat straight up.

"Keith, please get the door!" Mom shouted.

I jumped out of bed and ran down the stairs two at a time, launching myself off the last five or six steps and landing hard on the wood floor. I slid for a second in my socks, which was awesome, and then fell flat on my back. I just lay there staring up at the ceiling.

"Nice landing," Dad said, holding out a hand to help me up.

"Thanks, I thought I had it for a second."

"Yeah, you have to bend your knees to absorb the landing," Dad started to explain.

KNOCK, KNOCK, KNOCK!

"Keith! GET THE DOOR!" Mom shouted from the kitchen again.

"Okay!" I ran for the door and opened it. A guy in a huge rubber pencil costume was standing there next to a girl in a rubber book costume. They both looked miserable with the rain pouring down on them.

"DAD? Come quick, I don't know what this is!"

"We are a singing telegram for Keith Emerson," the pencil said.

I just looked at him. You know when you have no idea what is happening in a situation, and you can't even speak? That was what it was like. I wasn't even fully awake yet, and the pain from my fall had just reached my back.

Dad came running up with a tennis racket in his right hand ready to "serve" some trouble to whoever was at the front door.

"Hello, sir," the pencil said to my dad. "We're here to sing to Keith Emerson."

"We're a singing telegram," the lady in the book costume said in a low voice.

"Oh, I'm sorry! Come on in, it's miserable out there," Dad said putting the racket down. Mom and Emma had joined us at the door.

When Emma saw the pencil and the book, she bolted for her room. "I don't like that!" she shouted as she ran away. Emma has always been afraid of anyone in a costume.

"What in the world is this?" Mom asked.

Before I knew it, the pencil and the book burst into a shockingly bad song.

"Rise and shine,
You know you're a big boy.
Rise and shine,
You know you are a big boy!
BUT you're not as smart as you look,

NOOOO, you're not as smart as you look, look,
look!
So you better get a pencil,
Yeah, you better get a pencil,
And you better spend some time with a BOOK!
Because you're not as smart as you loooooooook.
After the IQ test,
you're gonna find
that it's your compaaaaany
that
Anthony
TOOOOOOOKKKKKKKK!"

They sang the last part really slow to make their point. Then they started the whole song all over again. My dad was laughing and trying to sing along, even though he didn't know the words. He looked at me and mouthed, "What's going on?"

Mom was frowning and looking confused, and I was just plain mad. Even so, I didn't want to yell at the pencil and the book; it wasn't their fault they had been hired to sing this song to me. So I waited until they were done, sporting a big fake smile on my face the whole time.

On the third time through the song, Dad yelled, "One more time!"

I looked at him in disbelief. He was quite a sight in his boxer shorts, black socks, and a shirt that read Fart Machine with his picture below it. Emma had bought the shirt for him on his birthday a few months back. It was pink, with purple hearts on it.

As I was taking in the image of Dad, the pencil held up a small video player and pressed the play button. It was Anthony. "Hi, Winderigheid," he said looking at the camera. "That means 'fart' in Dutch. I just wanted to send you off to school with a special song. Hope you have a great day at elementary school, big boy. Sir Anthony the Farter OVER AND OUT." Then he ripped two loud ones, and the camera went black.

"Sorry, kid," the pencil said. "I just put on the suit and sing the songs. The kid on the video doubled our pay to play the video." The book was already headed back to their car in the rain. The pencil followed.

I stood in the doorway with the rain pouring down and thought about the walk to the bus stop I'd have to make in a few minutes. I would have given anything to be home schooled at the lab like Anthony.

"I don't know what that was, but it was awesome!" Dad said, closing the door.

"You realize that was Anthony picking on me, don't you, Dad?"

He looked unsure. "It seemed to be in good fun. I think it's a pretty funny way to start the day. Maybe we can order a singing telegram for tomorrow, too."

CHAPTER 14

Career Week

By the time I made it to school, I was completely soaked. I hung my wet coat on the rack with all the others, walked into class, and took my seat. That ridiculous song was still in my head.

Scott rushed in and sat down. He looked like he had just climbed out of a swimming pool. You know when you're so completely soaked from the rain that even your sneakers have that squishy feeling? He looked like that.

He took out his morning work without even looking up at me.

"Hey," I said. "What's going on?"

"Nothing, what's up with you?"

"Nothing? You're drenched from head to toe! Are you really going to spend the rest of the day in those clothes?"

He looked down and seemed surprised that he was so wet. "Hey, you're right! I didn't realize it."

"Seriously? Are you okay?" I said.

"Yeah, I'm fine. I've just been up all night for the past few nights. I can't stop thinking about Virtual Reality Housing. It's starting to drive me crazy. I can see the idea in my head, but I can't figure out how to make it real." He did look really tired.

Mr. Cherub walked over to Scott's desk. "Scott, do you remember when we learned about liquids last year?"

"Yes, Mr. Cherub," Scott answered.

"Well, do you remember that people generally take precautions when it is raining? They usually wear a raincoat or use an umbrella of some kind."

"Ducks don't have to do that because their feathers have a natural oil that repels the water," Scott added.

"True! Good memory. Unfortunately, you are not a duck and you are making a puddle in my classroom. Please go down to the nurse and ask her to find you some dry clothes."

Just then Mr. Michaels, the principal, came over the loudspeaker. "Good morning, Harbor side Elementary. Unfortunately, we will not be serving chicken fingers today, because of a mix-up that I won't get into right now. In substitution, we will be serving hot dogs, again."

I groaned. I could just see Anthony at the lab ordering a pizza or making a gigantic sandwich with my turkey and cheese from the fridge. That was one of my favorite perks of working at the lab. We always had the kitchen stocked up with food. I missed my kitchen.

Mr. Michaels continued, "Also, I have an exciting announcement to make. A successful local businessman is coming in to talk with you all later this afternoon as part of career week." *Excellent! An assembly is not a bad way to waste a little time in the afternoon. Things are starting to look up,* I thought.

At least having Anthony away from school gave me a break from him for part of the day. Still, I should have been the one hanging out at the lab all day long with a private tutor, and he should be here sweating it out at elementary school, eating hot dogs for lunch.

The rest of the day went pretty smoothly. We had gym, the weather cleared up, and we were able to go out and play for recess. And to top it off, Mr. Cherub promised us that if we got all our work done before the assembly, we could have free time for the last forty-five minutes of the day.

I got all my work done and pushed Scott to get his work done, too. It was all planned out perfectly. We would go to the assembly, catch a little rest, and then head back to class for some free time until the end of the day. Not bad at all.

We were inline for the assembly when Mr. Cherub announced, "I want everyone to be on their best behavior today. Our visitor is taking time out of his busy schedule to talk with you all. Scott and Keith, I think you will really enjoy this."

CHAPTER 15

Sneak Attack

There wasn't time to ask Mr. Cherub what he meant before we had to sit down. Scott was hoping that the speaker was going to be a Yankees player, but I reminded him that it was a businessman.

Waiting there in my chair, I started feeling sleepy almost immediately. I knew once the auditorium lights went out, the lights would really go out for me. I don't know what it is about assemblies, but they always make me really sleepy.

After the last few classes came in and found their seats, the lights dimmed, and then went out almost completely. Only the stage was lit. It was perfect. I was already two or three yawns into my much-earned nap when Mr. Michaels walked out on stage and started talking about how important business was to our economy and blah, blah, blah.

I was getting sleepier by the minute, wishing that Scott had actually created those Virtual Reality Housing glasses, because I would have slapped on a pair and been sitting on a big comfy couch instead of in the stinky auditorium chair I was in. A virtual pillow and a blanket wouldn't have hurt either.

That was right about the time that Mr. Michaels recaptured my attention. "This visitor is a local businessman, a world traveler, and a bit of a math whiz. He's become so successful that he has taken control of his own education by hiring himself a private tutor."

This can't be.

"And as much as we all miss him, we are happy to welcome back Harbor side Elementary School's very own Anthony Papas."

Kids started clapping like mad, and Mr. Michaels looked about as proud as a peacock. Scott and I exchanged horrified looks, and then just shook our heads.

Anthony came strutting out on stage in a fancy suit. I must have been in shock, because I don't even remember what he said in those first few seconds.

By the time I refocused, Anthony was going on about his lottery experiment and how he found a pattern in the numbers that helped him predict the winning ticket. It was stuff we all knew about, but everyone seemed to still love hearing it, and Anthony certainly still loved telling it. He really dragged the whole thing out. I was just about done listening when he started talking about Sweet Farts.

"You see, kids, when you are running a major company like Sweet Farts, it's not all fun and games. You need to be serious about your work and getting things done. On my trip around the world, I learned a lot of things about people and business," he proclaimed, pacing around the stage like a college professor giving a lecture. "If you are going to get into a business, you have to have the time to put into it. For example, a child attending elementary school would not make a good company leader, because he would have to spend the entire day at school. A good leader needs to be with his company all day long to deal with things as they happen. That's one of the main reasons I hired myself a personal tutor. Sure, Keith Emerson is the leader of Sweet Farts in a lot of ways. But it's me who really runs the place."

I bit my knuckle to keep from screaming. I couldn't believe he was talking about the company as if it were his.

"I am excited to be here in front of you all today to share my business and scientific knowledge, and also to announce a little competition Keith and I are having to see who should run the company in the future. Do you guys like a little competition?" he asked, holding his hand to one ear and leaning toward the audience.

The kids all screamed and cheered, even though they had no idea what Anthony was talking about. Actually, I was somehow in this competition, and I didn't even know what he was talking about.

Scott stood up and shouted, "OOHHH YEAH! It's on!" as loud as he could. The crowd went nuts again. I held my hands up to Scott. *What are you doing to me, dude?* I thought. He looked back, shrugged, and then mouthed, "This is sooo exciting!"

Yeah, about as exciting as a heart attack, I thought. I'd had enough.

"Anthony," I announced in a loud voice, standing up. The room went silent. "We talked about this for a few minutes the other day at the lab. No one ever agreed to anything."

"Ladies and germs, the so-called 'president' of Sweet Farts, the great windstorm himself, KEITH EMERSON." The crowd cheered even louder.

I was embarrassed, but I sort of felt like a rock star at the same time. I waved and took a little bow. It seemed like the natural thing to do.

When the crowd quieted down again, I continued, "Anthony, you are forgetting that we didn't agree to anything." I felt like I was in an old-fashioned Western shoot-out.

"That's where you are wrong, my smelly friend. You told me to talk with Mr. Gonzalez and ask him about my challenge. Well, he said it was okay as long as we both agreed to it. So, students of Harbor side Elementary, you are the first kids anywhere to learn of the challenge I now put before Keith Emerson, the great inventor of Sweet Farts. Whoever has the highest IQ in the company shall become its new leader."

The crowd went nuts again. I turned toward Scott for some encouragement. Unfortunately, he was cheering along with the rest of the crowd so intensely that he didn't notice.

Mr. Michaels joined Anthony on stage and leaned into the microphone. "How exciting, kids! Can you believe these two geniuses? It isn't enough for them each to have had an amazing discovery at such a young age, but they want to challenge each other to a competition based on intelligence! I agree with Scott Castings, 'It's oooooon!'" he said in a low, wrestling-announcer voice. "Come on up here, Keith!"

The crowd went totally berserk.

I found myself walking down the aisle, up the stage steps, and toward Anthony and Mr. Michaels. My heart was racing. Mr. Michaels handed me the microphone.

"Hey," I said softly into the mike. Aside from a few giggles, the crowd fell silent. I think the audience could sense my fear. I should have said something like, *Yeah right, Anthony! You work for me and I am not going to take part in such a silly competition.* Or *Anthony, I think you are still recovering from your long trip around the world; of course, we aren't going to have a competition to see who runs my company.* But I didn't say any of those things. I don't know if it was all those years of Anthony teasing me and pushing me around or what, but something just clicked inside me and I was fired up. I raised my hand in the air and in a strong, clear voice yelled, "IT IS ON!"

The place went wild again. Teachers, students, even the lunch ladies were in the auditorium cheering. It felt pretty good, even though there was a part of me that knew this was probably the biggest mistake of my life.

Anthony took the microphone from my hand. Then he stood next to me facing the audience, grabbed my hand, and held it up high, like we were two Olympics medalists. He took a bow, and for some reason I did, too. I guess I was getting caught up in the excitement. In mid-bow, Anthony slipped the microphone behind him and let one rip. It echoed through the auditorium like a violent thunderclap.

"Come on, Farts! Can't you keep it under control for once in your life?" Anthony exclaimed, shaking his head in disgust, and then holding his nose and pointing at me.

The crowd went crazy with laughter, and I felt like I might just turn to dust right there on the stage. Anthony had blamed me for his gas a million times before, but this was worse. We were on stage in front of the whole school! I tried to get the microphone from him, but Mr. Michaels stepped in and took it from Anthony.

"Wow, Keith, we know you invented Sweet Farts, but you don't have to show off!" he said. The kids laughed even harder. "But seriously, let's not let that take away from this exciting challenge. May the smartest man win!" he announced, and the cheers continued.

Anthony leaned in real close to me and whispered, "I'm going to win this, Keith."

CHAPTER 16

Thanks, Alfred Binet

When we came back to our classroom after the assembly, I felt like my brain was on ice. Anthony had completely blindsided me. Not only did he really get me with the whole IQ challenge thing, but then he blamed one of his farts on me AGAIN! I couldn't believe it. He'd set that whole thing up, right down to the fart in the microphone.

During free time, I sat down at the computer to research IQ tests. Scott came over and tried to get me involved in a game, but I wasn't interested. Mr. Cherub came over and tried to cheer me up, but I was beyond cheering. The more I read, the more worried I became. These were tests on reasoning and thought process. Anthony might not be the smartest guy in the world but, I had to admit, he was clever. He had made me look ridiculous more times than I cared to remember. This IQ thing might be a bigger problem than I realized.

The Web site I was on said that IQ stands for Intelligence Quotient. I could barely understand half of what the article was saying, but I did understand that an IQ test is very complicated. This guy named Alfred Binet started testing kids using some test he created back in 1904, and there's some crazy method to determine the score.

I couldn't help but think that if Alfred Binet created the test to determine how smart people are, he must have been the smartest person in the world. I mean, how can one person create a test to determine how smart other people are unless the person creating the test is smarter than everyone else? I also wondered, what if Alfred Binet wasn't really all that smart after all, but everyone just thought he was smart because he created a test on smarts? I was getting myself even more confused. And while I kind of understood what the articles were saying, I couldn't have explained it to someone else.

Mr. Cherub always tells us that if we can explain something to someone else and help them understand it, then that means we truly understand it. I definitely could not explain an IQ test to someone else. And if I couldn't even explain how the test worked, how in the world could I expect to do well on it?

CHAPTER 17

Breakdown

Dad walked into my room later that night while I was lying on the bed, still in shock from the assembly.

"Hey, buddy, I just got off the phone with Mr. Cherub. Do you want to talk about what happened today?"

I could only shake my head back and forth. You know when you are so close to crying, and you are doing everything you can think of to keep from crying, but you know it's coming? That's where I was at that moment. I took a deep breath in, and then breathed out hard through my nose.

"We don't have to talk about it," he continued. "But from what Mr. Cherub said, it sounds like things got really crazy today at school. I know you and Anthony joke around a lot and give each other a hard time, but today sounded like it might have been different. Maybe you were right about the singing telegram the other day. I just figured you guys were playing around."

"I don't know how I always end up in these situations, Dad," I said through the tears that were now falling.

"Did you really agree to have an intelligence competition with Anthony?"

Before I could answer, Mom walked in. "I'm sooo sorry. What in the world happened today?" she asked, sitting down on the edge of my bed.

It's strange when you're that upset. You just don't know how your body is going to react. When I started thinking about everything that had taken place over the past few days, I couldn't help but laugh. Mom and Dad must have thought I was nuts because there I was laughing and crying at the same time.

"Keith, I thought you were upset. You were crying just a few seconds ago," Dad said.

I didn't even know why I was laughing. "I'm not sure; maybe I've just been embarrassed so many times that I'm over it already."

"That doesn't sound like you," my mom said. "I think you need to get some sleep." She kissed me on the forehead and gave me a hug. "I'm upset that Mr. Michaels let it get so out of control today."

"Mr. Michaels loves it when the kids get excited about something at school. I think he just got caught up in it like I did. I shouldn't have agreed to the challenge," I said.

"Yes, you let your emotions get the best of you," Mom said.

"The whole day feels like a bad dream. I'm being tortured by the mad flatulist."

"What in the world is a flatulist?" Mom asked.

"Oh, that's a person who can pass gas whenever they want," Dad said without missing a beat.

"How in the world do you know that?" Mom asked.

"Something I read, I guess. I think I came across it when I was researching the Amplifier." My mom groaned. The Amplifier was something Dad invented when he was working in the lab with me. It does exactly what its name suggests: it amplifies the sound of your gas. Dad loves it. Mom does not.

Dad wanted to have them made and sold in stores everywhere, but Mom convinced him that being famous for inventing Sweet Farts was embarrassing enough. He agreed, but kept one for himself. He didn't use it very often, but when he did, it was louder than a siren. One time I heard him rip one when I was outside playing basketball. He was in the house at the time and all the windows were closed!

He walked toward the door and let one go. It echoed for what seemed like eternity and then stopped in a loud squeak, like a bus with old brakes coming to a slow stop. "Hey, maybe I'm a flatulist, too!"

CHAPTER 18

They Fart All the Time

The next day at the lab I was in the kitchen getting a snack when I noticed a bus in the parking lot. There were no people in the lab who would have come on a bus, so I decided to walk out to Emma's petting zoo and see if they might be there.

Emma was there with Grandma, several scientists from the lab, and about twenty very old people. Some were in wheelchairs, some were walking with canes, and some were sitting on chairs.

Grandma was wearing a white lab coat and looked like she might know what was happening. "Hey, Grandma, what's going on here? Why are all these…ummm…people here?"

"Why are all these ummm people here? It's okay to say *old people,* Keith. They are old. It's part of life."

"What are they doing here?" I asked.

"Why don't you ask your sister?"

Emma came running up. She was holding a baby chick. "Hi, Keith, want to play with the bunnies yet? They are over there by Mrs. Smeltz, the lady in the wheelchair."

"No thanks, Emma. But who are all these people?"

"They're from the place that I went to on my field trip."

"Emma went to the retirement home the other day with her class," Grandma said.

"Okay, but why are they here?" I asked.

"Because they're my friends. When I went to visit them, it was so boring. I invited them to come to play with the bunnies, and they said YES!" Emma said. "Can I hire them, too?"

"You want to hire all these old people?"

"Yep, I want to hire all of them, and Jonathan and Ruby." She pointed to her friends as if I hadn't met them before. Jonathan was throwing a ball with Goofy, and Ruby was sitting next to an old lady on a bench. They each had a bunny on their laps, and they were laughing about something. "These people are really nice, Keith, and they have lots of free time. They said they can come here every day."

"I'm sorry, Emm, we can't hire these people to work at Sweet Farts. I'm still trying to manage the people I have already."

"You should really think about it. They're perfect for your company." She smiled and whispered, "They fart all the time."

CHAPTER 19

Back to the Lab Already!

I heard Anthony cannon-balling in his pool as I walked into my lab. I thought about going over and trying to talk some sense into him, but decided my time was better spent working. The AWSC was only a few weeks away. Scott was working on his Virtual Reality Housing project, Anthony was working on destroying my company, Emma was playing out back with animals and old people, and I was without an idea…again!

"How's it coming, Keith?" Mr. Stuart asked, pulling up a chair next to me.

"I'm sorry I didn't get you those scents yet. I've just had a lot on my mind, and I want to make sure that the new scents are original and interesting."

"It's okay, Keith. I just don't want it to creep up on you. The summer is coming faster than you think. More importantly, those Liver Cane samples we worked on the other day are not too bad. Have you tried them yet?"

"I haven't," I said. "You would think I'd be excited that we're getting close, but I think I'm tired of working on something that I can't seem to solve. It feels like we'll never get them right."

"Keith, you were spoiled a bit when we helped you invent Sweet Farts. That was an amazingly fast amount of time to invent something so useful. Science is not about speed; it is about persistence and time."

"What's persistence?" I asked.

"Persistence is continuing to work on something even when you might not want to. It's a fancy word for not giving up. Without persistence, you can't be a scientist. Be patient. We'll get it sooner or later."

"I kind of need sooner. The AWSC is in a few weeks, and I'm not sure what I'm going to present."

"You'll present what you have. If you don't reach your goal, you'll keep working until you do. That's what science is all about. Mr. Gonzalez doesn't expect you to win every time, Keith. He does expect you to try your best every time, though. I think you can give him that."

Mr. Stuart was making a lot of sense. Even though I didn't have the Liver Canes perfected, I had an idea that I believed in. Someday, the world would enjoy candy that had all the nutrients of healthy food.

CHAPTER 20

The Clock Is Ticking

The next day Mr. Gonzalez called a meeting. Anthony, Scott, Emma, Grandma, and I sat around the big baseball table. It was really quiet. Anthony and I hadn't seen much of each other since the "guest visitor" event at school. To my surprise, Mr. Gonzalez had also invited Mr. Michaels and Mr. Cherub to the meeting.

Mr. Gonzalez stood and pushed his chair in. "Hello, everyone. I called you all here to talk about the state of your company. Keith, you came up with the idea for Sweet Farts, and it has been a great success. People around the world no longer have to smell the terrible scent of human gas because of your idea. Anthony, you had an amazing discovery in number patterns last year. You applied that work to the lottery and proved that it can be predicted. Your work has helped scientists understand random numbers in a way they never could before. You should both be very proud of your accomplishments; however, I can't say I'm happy with the way things have been going lately."

I took a deep breath.

"Mr. Gonzalez, if I may," Anthony said, starting to stand.

"Anthony, please stay seated. I don't want to hear again about how you think you should run the company. I've had enough of your bickering and negative attitudes toward each other."

"I told you how nasty Anthony can be," I said, wondering if he was finally about to fire him.

"I don't want to hear any complaining from you either, Keith." I had never heard Mr. Gonzalez like this before. He was usually so laid back and relaxed.

"Mr. Michaels called me the other day to tell me about the nonsense that went on at your school assembly. I'm very frustrated that neither of you decided to tell me the stakes of this IQ challenge. Furthermore, I find it fascinating that you guys have been given all this opportunity, and the one thing that you have chosen to focus on is being in charge! This lab is not about power. This lab is about science." He paced around the table.

"Anthony, what did I tell you when you came to me and asked if I would allow an IQ challenge?

I had never seen Anthony so quiet. He looked like a dog that just peed on the new carpet.

Mr. Gonzalez continued, "I told you that what we do here isn't about your IQ. It is about creativity and trying to make the world a better place. The results of a test can't determine who is smarter. People are smart in many, many different ways. Doing well on a test is one kind of intelligence, but there are countless other kinds. And to even suggest using an intelligence test to determine who should run a company only reminds me of how young you two really are."

He turned to me and added, "Keith, when you were in here complaining to me about Anthony and the way he treats you, I told you that you needed to stand up for yourself. That assembly would have been the perfect time to do that. Instead, you got sucked right in."

My face got all hot, and I couldn't meet his eyes. I knew Mr. Gonzalez was right. I should have stood up for myself.

"Well, gentlemen, you know the saying, 'Be careful what you wish for, you just might get it.' Since you two geniuses decided it would be a good idea to have a competition to see who should be running Sweet Farts, that is exactly what you are going to get."

"You're going to let us have the IQ challenge?" Anthony asked, perking up.

"No. But I do think a little healthy competition might be just what you kids need. Mr. Michaels, will you please explain?"

Mr. Michaels stood, cleared his throat, and straightened his tie. "Okay, so things got a little out of control the other day. Obviously, I thought you boys had cleared all this with Mr. Gonzalez before announcing it to the entire school. Regardless, everyone feels that you gentlemen have had your priorities in the wrong place lately. So, in an attempt to get you two back on track, we have decided that whoever's work is chosen for presentation at the AWSC will also become the new head of Sweet Farts, Inc."

"Can I be part of this, too?" Scott asked.

"Yes, you are part of this company," Mr. Gonzalez answered.

"That's not fair," Anthony blurted out. I was thinking the same thing, but I was glad I wasn't the one that said it.

"Why?" he asked.

"Because the challenge is supposed to be between me and Keith, not Scott, and certainly not Emma!"

"I don't even want to be in your silly competition, Anthony," Emma shot back. "All you care about is being the best."

"Okay, so you're not in the challenge, and neither is Scott," Anthony declared.

"Excuse me, Anthony," Mr. Gonzalez replied. "You are getting a little ahead of yourself. You and Keith wanted a competition that would decide who should be running this company, and that includes Scott and Emma. I want to give you kids as much control as you can handle, but I cannot, and will not, allow you to embarrass me and my scientists with your childish games. So, it is decided, you will *all* be judged on the scientific work you complete between now and the AWSC, and the winner takes it all."

CHAPTER 21

Poop Field

Later that day, I headed to the batting cages. I took a few halfhearted swings. I couldn't believe I might lose control of the company. It was hard to imagine Anthony running things. As deep as I was in my thoughts, I couldn't help but notice there was a weird smell in the air. I kept getting a whiff of it every time the breeze picked up. It was definitely poop.

I peeked over the fence between the batting cages and Emma's petting zoo. There was another bus parked in the distance and a bunch of kids hanging out with Emma again. I hopped the fence in one jump. I love how I can easily jump over a fence. I always worry that I'm going to fall or catch myself on the fence, but it never happens.

Walking up, I noticed each of the kids was holding or playing with one of Emma's animals. There were bunnies, goats, chicks, kittens, puppies—it was crazy. Goofy ran up and jumped on me. It seemed every time I visited Emma's barn more animals were running around. But there were a lot of scientists out there, too.

"Hi, Keith, ready to play with bunnies yet?" Emma asked.

"No. I came over because I can smell the poop from the other side of the fence. You have to clean up after them better," I said, trying to keep Goofy from jumping up on me.

Mr. Gonzalez startled me by putting his hand on my shoulder. I hadn't seen him standing there.

"Keith, Emma is taking care of her animals just fine," he said.

"But they stink, and I keep finding some kind of poop on my field."

"That's probably the goats," Emma said. "They like to graze. The grass on your field is their favorite. It's different than the grass I have over here." She turned and walked away.

Mr. Gonzalez just smiled.

"Why are you smiling?" I asked.

"I just find it wonderful that your sister knows so much about her animals. Don't you?"

A little boy in an arm cast was sitting on the grass by himself. Emma walked up to him and grabbed his good hand. "Come on, Robbie, I got a baby lamb this morning. He is sooo cuddly." The two of them walked over to the barn that had been built to help house all of Emma's animals.

Mr. Gonzalez started toward Grandma, and I chased after him. "Mr. Gonzalez, do you really think it's a good idea for Emma to have all these animals out here? I mean, it looks like your scientists are turning into farmers to keep up with it all. She's got so many animals—chicks, goats, kittens, puppies, and…a lamb?"

"Don't forget bunnies, ferrets, gerbils, and a miniature pony," Grandma added. She checked something off on the clipboard in her hand.

"Really? Isn't that a little crazy?" I asked. She handed the clipboard to Mr. Gonzalez, who checked something off and handed it back to her.

"Keith, what have you been working on in the lab lately?" Mr. Gonzalez asked.

"I'm pretty close to perfecting Liver Canes. I made some the other day that were really close.

Mr. Stuart is helping me, and I'm pretty on top of it," I replied, stretching the truth a bit.

"Well, Emma is just getting started. Just like you, she'll be given time to set her space up as she sees fit."

"Yeah, but all the animals? And the poop? It doesn't seem very clean. Also, she just seems to be having play dates. Did you know she had a bunch of old people here the other day?"

"Of course I do, Keith. They are coming back tomorrow, I believe," Mr. Gonzalez said.

"They're coming in the morning, and there's another group from a different retirement center coming in the afternoon," Grandma said, flipping the page on her clipboard.

Emma walked back out to the grass with Robbie and the baby lamb. The rest of the kids came over to pet it. They were all sitting on the ground, petting the lamb, giggling, and smiling.

"What is going on out here?" I asked Mr. Gonzalez.

"More than you realize," Mr. Gonzalez said mysteriously.

CHAPTER 22
Let's Go!

The next day was the All-World Science Challenge orientation. It was a chance to meet some of the other kids and allow the judges to get an idea of the work that would be presented on the day of the challenge. Sweet Farts didn't display anything for the orientation. We only went so we could get an idea of what the real event would be like.

Mr. Gonzalez had scheduled a van to take all of us into New York City that day. It was to arrive at my house at six a.m. in order to miss the morning traffic. I was glad we were leaving early because it was raining again, and when it rains in New York, the traffic goes from bad to insane. It has always amazed me that the drive to New York

City, which usually takes an hour, can take almost three hours when the traffic is bad.

I scooped up the last of my yogurt and shouted, "EMMA! Let's go."

Mom walked into the kitchen. "Keith, why are you screaming?"

"I want to get going. I'm anxious to see what the AWSC is all about. I wish you and Dad could come."

"I wish we could, too. You'll tell me all about it tonight."

Mom had started picking up shifts at her old job ever since I made my "we-should-get-a-bigger-house" comment. I think it bothered my parents that they couldn't afford a larger place. I wish they would just let me buy a new house for us.

"Mom, you really don't have to go to work anymore. I want you and Dad to use some of the Sweet Farts money."

"Keith, you know your father and I are not going to use your money to pay for our family expenses. Your father and I have been talking about buying a bigger house someday, though, long before you made your suggestion. Maybe one day soon we'll get that bigger house. But we'll get it because your dad and I decided it was time."

Mom had been a nurse at the hospital before Emma and I came along. She worked on the floor that delivered the babies. We went there with her sometimes to visit her nurse friends.

"Mom, why don't you work for Sweet Farts? You can help out at the lab and…"

"Keith, it's okay. I like my work. It's sweet that you want to help out, but I can't take your money, and I definitely can't work for you."

I spotted a white van pulling up the driveway. "Suit yourself. EMMMMMAAAAAA!" I shouted. "The van is here."

CHAPTER 23

Someone Made a Poop in the Van

The rain was coming down, and I had to put my hood up as I rushed to the van. The music was so loud I could hear it from outside the van. It was my favorite band, Turpentine Fire Line, playing their new song, "Ghost Ride." That meant one thing.

"Good morning, Grandma," I shouted, opening the van door. "I didn't know you were driving us."

"Who did you think was? I'm not going to let just anybody drive my precious cargo to the city. We're going to have fun today," she shouted back.

"I don't know. You are aware that we're picking Anthony up, right?"

She turned the radio down. "Mr. Gonzalez told me. It will be fine. You two need to put your issues aside and get on the same team already."

"Trust me, I've tried."

"Well, keep trying."

Emma climbed into the van. "Gross! This weather is terrible."

"Good morning, Sunshine Face," Grandma said. I was always amazed at how upbeat Grandma could be. It was the crack of dawn, and we were about to go on a rainy, traffic-filled ride to the city, but you would have thought she was driving us to the beach on a sunny day. With Grandma, the weather didn't matter; her mood stayed the same. It was one of the things I loved most about her.

The van had two rows. I sat right behind Grandma, and Emma sat next to me; at least Anthony wouldn't be able to sit next to me. Grandma turned the radio down and waved to Mom as we pulled away.

"So are you excited to go learn about the All-World Science Challenge?" she asked.

"I am," Emma replied. "Mom said they would probably have lots of snacks there. Mr. Gonzalez said there would be a lot of animals, too."

We pulled up in front of Scott's house. He came running out through the pouring rain. Again, he didn't have on a raincoat or an umbrella with him. By the time he had climbed into the van, he was soaked.

Scott was shaking with the chills when we got to Anthony's house. "Too bad you can't make virtual reality clothes," I said.

"Yeah, that would be awesome. Maybe I'll get to work on that."

Anthony climbed into the van, slid back behind me, and sat next to Scott. I didn't say anything and neither did he. Grandma turned the radio down even lower.

"Well this is fun," Emma finally said.

"Yeah," Scott added. "How long are you guys going to stay mad at each other?"

"I'm not mad at anyone," Anthony said, as if he didn't even know I was mad. "Who's mad? What are you talking about?"

"Come on, Anthony!" I said, turning around to face him. "You really expect me to believe that you don't know I'm still mad about what you did at school?"

Anthony looked at Scott and shrugged. "Should I have known that? How would I know that, Keith? You haven't told me. I may be brilliant, but I'm not a mind reader."

"Do you have any idea how embarrassing that was? It was in front of the whole school!"

"Keith, I was kidding. It was a joke. In case you haven't noticed, I like to joke around."

"Yeah, so do I, but you're always embarrassing me and making people think I'm farting when I'm not."

"Who cares what they think? You are the inventor of Sweet Farts. What do you care if a bunch of kids at school think you're a fart machine?"

I glanced up at Grandma, who was pretending she wasn't listening. I turned back to face Anthony. "Because I am not a fart machine. You are."

"Yeah, but it's so much fun making people think it's you. The way you get sooo upset, it's ridiculous. You need to toughen up already. You are the president of a very successful company, but you don't act like it. That is why I feel I should..."

"We know, Anthony," Scott interrupted, "you want to take over the company. You guys are unbelievable. You both have made these cool discoveries. You both have your own spots at Mr. Gonzalez's lab. You both have lots of money. But you can't have fun with it. Do you even understand how cool the lab is?"

"Yeah," Emma added. "When I was little I wanted to be a part of the company so badly. Now that I'm in it, I realize you guys argue more than the kids in my class. It's kind of lame."

I couldn't believe Emma had just called us lame. It seemed like just yesterday she was talking like a baby and now she was becoming part of the group. "Emma, we're not lame. We're just having a hard time getting along."

"I agree with Emma. You guys are being pretty lame," Grandma shouted, turning Turpentine Fire Line way up.

What a great way to start the morning. Standing up to Anthony hadn't worked, and now Grandma and Emma thought I was lame.

No one said anything for a while after that. We still had a long way to go until we reached the city. We were on the expressway and we were already in traffic. I was staring out the window, watching the cars next to us crawl forward, when I got a whiff of Anthony.

"Come on, man!" Scott shouted and held his nose.

"EWWWW!" Emma screamed. "Someone pooped in here! Someone made a poop in the van, Grandma!"

"I'm pretty sure no one pooped, Emma. Unless, of course, you snuck a few bunnies into the van," Grandma said.

"Emma," I said. "It was Anthony. He doesn't take Sweet Farts tablets, so he smells like a barn."

"Keith, don't try to blame it on me," Anthony replied.

"Anthony, that is disgusting," Emma scolded.

"Sorry to be the one to tell you this, Emm," he said. "It's your brother. He doesn't even take his own Sweet Farts tablets. It's pretty gross if you ask me."

Emma turned back to look at me. She was holding her nose. "Keith, did you make that horrible smell?"

"NO!" I said. "Of course I didn't. Anthony has been doing this to me since last year. He is a flatulist; he farts when he wants to. You can't seriously think that was me."

The whole rest of the trip I tried to convince Emma that it wasn't me, but she wasn't totally buying it.

"Why does everyone have such a hard time believing that I am not a farter?"

No one answered.

CHAPTER 24

The Blue-ringed Octopus

I couldn't believe how many people were at the convention center. It was this massive building that reminded me of the mall, but without the stores. There were tables set up all over the place and kids busy preparing their displays. Every table featured colorful banners and posters. All of us got to wear a badge that had Sweet Farts written on it.

Since we weren't setting up our own booth, we decided to walk around and see what the competition was all about. We passed table after table of kids with all kinds of cool stuff. There were electronics, machines, things bubbling, boiling, blasting, smashing—it seemed to go on forever.

Then we came to a booth with a bunch of fish tanks set up. Each tank had at least one octopus in it. Emma and I were looking at one of them when this kid with huge black glasses walked up next to us and said, "It's awesome isn't it?"

"Yeah," I said. It was awesome. The octopus had crazy blue circles on it. I had never seen anything like it.

"It's beautiful," Emma said.

"Yeah," the kid said back. "But it can kill you."

"No it can't," I heard Anthony say.

The kid just looked at Anthony. "It most certainly can. I raised it myself. It's a blue-ringed octopus."

"Well, it can't kill you. It's not even that big," Anthony argued.

"Okay, then stick your hand in and grab it," Scott suggested.

Immediately, Anthony started rolling up his sleeves. The kid with the glasses grinned.

Emma tapped me on the shoulder. "Not now, Emma, this is too good."

She tapped harder. "What?" I finally asked.

She just pointed to the poster on the wall behind the table. It read, "Kyle Farnesworth: Deadly Octopus Exhibit." I looked at Anthony.

He already had his hand in the water and was reaching for the blue-ringed octopus. Kyle's smile widened. Scott was so excited he was jumping up and down.

"NOOOO!" I shouted, pulling Anthony's arm back and out of the tank.

Anthony tried to resist, but I was able to get his hand out safely. "What's your problem, Keith?"

Emma pointed to the poster on the wall again and shook her head. "You boys aren't very bright."

"You were going to let me get killed?" Anthony shouted at the octopus kid.

"Of course not," Kyle said. "I'm working on an antidote to their venomous sting. I would have given you something that would have probably saved you."

"*Probably* saved me?"

"Yeah, it's hard to test my antidote because people don't get stung by them very often. But I'm almost positive you would have lived."

It's not very often that Anthony is at a loss for words. But he just stood there glaring at the kid. Kyle was just looking right back at him, and finally said, "Well, are you going to stick your hand in or not? My antivenom isn't going to invent itself."

CHAPTER 25

We Might Be Lame

The more I walked around, the more I realized how amazing the AWSC was. There were kids from all over the world. There were kids who were already taking college-level classes in fifth and sixth grade. There were kids who had made inventions that helped people with diseases. We even met a team that was working with NASA. This was no school science fair. This was the big leagues.

Maybe Sweet Farts wasn't so amazing, after all. I mean, farts are a problem, but there are much bigger ones out there. And Anthony's lottery code was cool, but aside from the money he donated, it only helped him and no one else.

I think we were all feeling a little embarrassed as we walked around the convention center.

There were so many kids with so many amazing projects, and we had nothing to share. I even think Anthony was feeling a little embarrassed, because I overheard him say to some kid at one of the tables, "I have lots of great stuff I'm working on at the lab right now. It's just that I was traveling the world for the past few months."

"Was the travel part of your project?" the boy asked.

"No, it was for relaxation," Anthony said. I noticed that he left out the fact that his trip was inspired by his love for saying the word *fart* in other languages.

And there were so many exhibits that involved animals, it made me a little jealous that I hadn't thought to get some really cool animals and keep them in my lab. Not bunnies and goats like Emma had—boa constrictors, pythons, and maybe a tiger. *How awesome would that be to have a tiger at the lab!*

Maybe Emma had the right idea from the start. She liked animals, so she had lots of animals at the lab. Sure, she wasn't doing any science, but she was only five. Back when Mr. Gonzalez invited me to be a part of his lab, he said I could study anything I wanted, and I built a baseball field and a basketball court. No wonder Mr. Gonzalez was so frustrated with us. He expected more.

"I think Emma might be right. We might be lame," I said to Scott.

"Why? Because you haven't stood up to Anthony yet?"

"What do you mean? I always stand up to Anthony."

"You complain about Anthony, but I don't think what you do could be considered standing up to him. But if you're not feeling lame about that, what are you feeling lame about?"

"This place. I feel like all these kids are doing such cool science. I wish I were doing something amazing."

"You are. You're trying to make healthy food taste awesome. If you can pull that off, you'll be every kid's hero," Scott said.

"Yeah, but I haven't been working as hard as I should be. Mr. Gonzalez gave us the freedom to do whatever we wanted, and I kind of feel like we let him down."

"Well, thankfully he's not here because he would probably hire a bunch of other kid geniuses to work in our labs and have us cleaning the toilets in no time," Scott joked.

"No kidding! We really need to get on the ball. Do you think you'll have something to enter in the challenge?" I asked.

"I hope so. We still have a few weeks. It's got to be better than the tornado in a bottle I did last time."

CHAPTER 26

Leave It to the Guys

The bus ride back to the lab took longer than the ride in. There's not much worse than the trip home from the city in the rain and traffic. You feel as if you are never going to make it.

Anthony was snoring in the back seat. His tongue was hanging out and he was making loud snarling noises. Every so often, he would open and close his mouth so that it sounded like someone chewing with his mouth open. It was so loud and gross that I felt like I might throw up. He even mumbled a few times. I couldn't make out what he was saying, but I definitely think I heard the word *octopus*.

"Are you going to do anything for the challenge, Emma?"

"No, I'm not really interested in that stuff. I just want to share my animals with people. I'm thinking about what I should get next. Maybe one of those blue octopuses."

"Why would you want one of those? They're deadly."

"I wouldn't touch it. I'd keep it in a tank. I think the people at the retirement home would love the blue rings. Also, Robbie, the boy with the cast, would love it. I feel bad for him. He had arm surgery and is going to be in the hospital for a long time. He likes blue. It's his favorite color."

"What do you mean? The hospital?"

"A lot of the kids who come to visit the animals are from the hospital."

"I didn't know that, Emm. Why have you been having the kids from the hospital out to visit the animals?"

"Because I want to help them feel better and cheer them up."

"Wow. I know I've been giving you a hard time about the animals, but it's great that you set up your little petting zoo."

"It's not a petting zoo, Keith. It's a Smile Farm. Everyone that comes out there ends up smiling. Even you."

"Yeah, the animals are pretty awesome. Don't worry about doing a project for the AWSC, Emm. Leave it to the guys. One of us will have something great to present. Maybe you can enter in a few years when you're older. For now, just have fun with your animals like you've been doing."

Emma just gave me a funny smile.

CHAPTER 27

Almost There

The weeks that followed were extremely busy. We all worked in our labs every free minute. Emma was always hanging out back at her little farm, and Scott, Anthony, and I were hidden away in our labs trying to come up with an amazing invention to present at the AWSC. The three of us would run into each other out on the court or batting cage when we took a quick break, but no one was saying anything about how their project was going. There was just too much on the line.

Once a week we had our meeting, and once a week Scott reported that Virtual Reality Housing was coming along, but he had nothing to show yet. Anthony kept telling me he would be running things soon. And Emma talked on and on about her animals, and how she had invited people from hospitals and retirement homes. Emma definitely seemed to be having the most fun. The guys and I started hanging out back there a bit, too. At least once a day, I went to see the animals. They helped me take my mind off the pressure of the AWSC.

CHAPTER 28

Rise of the Emmpire

After weeks and weeks of work at the lab, the AWSC finally arrived. Mr. Gonzalez called the team together in the conference area. All the adults were there, too.

"This has been an interesting past few weeks for me," Mr. Gonzalez began. "I have watched you grow, and I have also watched you refuse to grow. I have to admit that I feel that some of you wasted a great deal of time during the first few weeks of this process. With that being said, I want to make sure we all understand what is going to happen next. Only one of your projects will be entered in the AWSC. Once that project is announced, the rest of you will support that project as your company's best work. Are there any questions?"

No one said a word.

"You are encouraged to continue working on your experiment, and to perhaps enter it in a contest like this another time. But for now, only one project may be entered. Mr. Michaels, Mr. Cherub, Grandma, and I have met several times to decide the winner."

"How did we do?" I asked sheepishly.

"Most of you did fine. There was one person who clearly stood out, though. This person surprised us all. I want to remind you guys that before we reveal the winner and new president of the company, you must agree to take the news in an appropriate way. You must show respect for the winner, as well as the losers. No name calling, no teasing, and the next time one of you goes and pulls a public prank," here he paused and looked at Anthony, "will be your last day at the lab. Am I making myself clear?"

We all nodded and held our breath. That is, all of us except Emma, who didn't seem to care one way or the other. Mr. Cuddlesworth didn't seem too concerned either.

Mr. Gonzalez continued, "After talking long and hard with some other scientists and your families, I have decided to only tell you the

winner's name. I am not going to get into who
came in second, third, and fourth. It could very
well have been any of you that scored fourth out
of four, and the way some of you have been acting
lately, I don't know that I can trust you to not tease
one another."

Scott winked at me and whispered, "That's
cool of him. He doesn't want to hurt Emma's
feelings."

"Scott, when you whisper in a silent room,
you may as well speak normally, because your
whispers are overheard, and then everyone is just
plain uncomfortable," Mr. Gonzalez said.

"Sorry," Scott said, pulling the pair of virtual
reality glasses down from his head to cover his eyes.

Mr. Gonzalez continued, "Thank you. Now,
the interesting thing about what you just said is
that Emma is not going to have to worry about
her feelings being hurt, because Emma happens
to be the winner." Mr. Gonzalez walked over to
where Emma was sitting. "Emma, I always knew
you were one of a kind, but I had no idea you were
this bright. You show signs of genius!"

Emma didn't look surprised. She smiled and
kept on petting her bunny. "I know," she said, like
it was no big deal.

"What?" I started. "But, Mr. Gonzalez, you can't really expect Emma to be in charge of the company. She's only five."

"I'm aware of how old she is. I am also aware of the way you boys have been handling things lately. I think it will do you guys some good to focus on science for a while and not worry about being in charge. Emma will have plenty of support from your parents, Grandma, and me. You gentlemen need only worry about your science."

"That, and listen to me and Mr. Cuddlesworth!" Emma said, laughing.

As I sat there watching everyone congratulate Emma, I realized I didn't feel angry or sad. I felt relieved. I felt relieved to not be in charge anymore, and even more relieved to know that Anthony wouldn't be taking over the company.

"I have met separately with all of you about your projects," Mr. Gonzalez said, turning to the rest of us. "Keith is coming along nicely with his molecular gastronomy project. Scott is finally getting some work done, and I am curious to see where his virtual-reality project takes him. Anthony, would you like to tell everyone what your situation is?"

Anthony looked uncomfortable. "Well, I kind of lost track of time these past few weeks. I have been just hanging out over in my lab since I came back. I don't have anything going on. Although I can do a jackknife, a flip, and a seriously big cannonball in the pool."

"And you wanted to run things?" I asked.

"I figured I would win the IQ test and I would- n't have to do anymore projects. I thought I could just manage you guys. Who knew Mr. Gonzalez would squash the IQ challenge and that your little sister was some sort of genius?"

"I did," Grandma said.

"Me too," Mom added.

"Yep, she's just like her dear old dad," Dad said, as he gave Emma a hug.

"Anthony and I have talked about it, and if he doesn't have a project up and running in the next month, he is out," Mr. Gonzalez said sternly. "Also, his home school days are over. He will be joining you guys at Harbor side Elementary starting next week."

"I would like to officially offer Mrs. Weaver a job tutoring me!" I said eagerly.

"I don't think so, Keith. The only one who is going to be home schooled around here is Emma.

Mrs. Weaver and Grandma will be working with her in the lab so she can continue her science work."

I almost fell out of my seat. Emma had not only won the challenge and taken over the company, but she was also going to live my dream of being schooled at the lab.

"Mom, I thought you said I couldn't be home schooled at the lab?" I asked.

"I did say you couldn't, but I think it will be a wonderful experience for Emma."

"It's going to be tough, but somebody has to do it!" Emma said.

We all laughed.

Mr. Gonzalez said, "You gentlemen should take a bit of advice from young Emma. She has been doing amazing work."

Anthony grumbled.

"Oh get over yourself, Anthony," I said. "Let's hear all about it, Emm." I *was* really excited for her. She looked so happy, and Mom, Dad, and Grandma were beaming. It reminded me how I felt when I invented Sweet Farts. Emma was happy for me back then, and I guess it was time for me to be happy for her now.

Emma stood up. "Well, ummm, the thing is...I don't really know what I did." She looked at Grandma.

"Sure you do, Emma. You have been doing great science the past few months. You were having so much fun you just didn't realize it. Tell everyone what you told me about cute baby animals and people."

"Oh that? I said that cute baby animals make people happy."

"Okay, and what did you ask if you could do?" Grandma added.

"I asked if I could share the baby animals with older people and people who feel sick."

"Exactly, and why did you want to do that?" Grandma asked.

"I wanted to do that because I knew it would make them feel better."

"I get it," I said. "That was your hypothesis! You predicted that older people and people who are feeling sick would feel better if they spent time with baby animals."

"Yeah, so?" Emma asked.

"So," Mr. Gonzalez continued. "That is how science works. You make a hypothesis, or a guess, about what you think will happen, and then you try it out and record what actually happens."

"So what happened?" Scott asked.

"You will just have to wait for the AWSC and see for yourself," Mr. Gonzalez replied. "I have one more surprise for you all. *The Helen Winifred Show* has been interested in what you are all up to. She invited you back to share your work and talk about the AWSC the day after the competition!"

CHAPTER 29

Passing the Torch

The day of the All-World Science Competition was really relaxing, actually. For once, I wasn't the center of attention. Emma seemed to handle the pressure much better than I did. I'm always a nervous wreck when I'm the center of attention. Emma didn't seem to mind it at all.

We all took a limousine into the city, while some of the scientists from the lab followed behind in a truck full of animals and materials for Emma's display. When we arrived, there was a huge booth toward the middle of the convention center. On the wall behind our table a big banner read *Sweet Farts, Inc.* The walls around the display were covered with thank-you letters to Emma from people she'd invited to her Smile Farm. I was amazed at how many people had written. The convention center was packed.

Most of Emma's animals were set up in a makeshift petting zoo or Smile Farm. Within minutes, there were people asking questions and talking with all of us. It went on like this for hours.

I found myself talking about the molecular gastronomy project a lot, and I saw Scott talking with kids about his Virtual Reality Housing idea. Anthony was bragging all day long about last year's lottery discovery. He was even complaining about how he couldn't spend all his money now; he had to wait until he was eighteen like me.

People were even asking Grandma about Square Fruit. Toward the end of the day, we all went into this huge auditorium. It must have held a thousand people. This was a much bigger audience than the one I announced Sweet Farts to. Emma had gone backstage with Grandma, Mom, Mr. Gonzalez, and some of the lab scientists. I hoped she wasn't too nervous.

Tons of kids presented their ideas. We saw projects on medicines, animals, plants—the list went on and on. I was amazed at some of the stuff these kids had worked on. In the end, the kid who won had built a rocket that reached outer space! He showed videos and pictures of his work that absolutely amazed me. As the winner of the AWSC, his project would be funded for the next ten years. And he didn't have to go to school anymore. His research was going to count toward his education since he would be working with world-class scientists at NASA.

At the very end of the ceremony, the announcer said, "Ladies and gentlemen, it is the distinct honor and privilege of the AWSC to introduce our youngest entrant ever. She may not have won this year, but I think you are getting an early look at a future science star. Please join me in welcoming Emma Emerson."

People were clapping like crazy when Emma walked out on stage with Mr. Gonzalez. She looked so tiny up there. I was amazed at how calm she was. She had a huge smile on her face and was blowing kisses. The host of the competition spoke into the microphone. "Hi, Emma, we are so proud to have you with us today."

"Thanks, I'm happy to be here," Emma said.

"Can you tell us about your project?" he asked. Emma went on to explain her project. The crowd seemed to really enjoy it. Then she got to the part that Scott, Anthony, and I didn't know about. Emma said, "I knew animals would make people feel happy. So I wanted to see if there was a type of animal that made people the happiest."

"So what did you do?" he asked.

"I set up a Smile Farm at the Sweet Farts labs. I collected all kinds of animals. They're so cute."

Mr. Gonzalez interrupted. "Emma went beyond simply playing with animals, which is what some of her colleagues thought she was doing. She had the scientists tracking which animals people responded to best. She tested the elderly, the young, and people dealing with illness and injury, and reached the same conclusion every time. Go ahead and tell them, Emma."

"The animal that makes people the most happy is the bunny."

Mr. Gonzalez continued, "Our scientists asked the people visiting Emma's Smile Farm questions about their happiness before they arrived. Then they interviewed them after visiting with the animals and Emma. What they overwhelmingly observed was that the people who interacted with the bunnies were happier and less stressed when they left than when they arrived."

"I knew it would end up that way," Emma announced. People laughed and started clapping. She couldn't have been cuter.

The announcer continued, "Emma's fantastic work and vision are going to be put to good use this coming summer when hundreds of hospitals and senior centers around the world build Smile Farms of their own. As our young scientist, Emma Emerson has proven that laughter is the best medicine."

Emma spoke into the microphone. "Keith, you need to play with bunnies. You won't worry so much." Then her friends John and Ruby, who were sitting up front, started the chant, "Play with bunnies, play with bunnies, play with bunnies." Oddly enough, the crowd started chanting along with them. I couldn't believe it, but I found myself chanting right along with them.

CHAPTER 30

The Helen Winifred Show №2

The Helen Winifred Show was sometimes taped at different locations around the city. The day we were on, it was being taped at Yankee Stadium, right before a game. I was so excited. Mr. Gonzalez told us that Helen herself had decided to tape the show at the game in our honor. She knew how much of a fan I was.

We arrived early and got to meet some of the players; I got a few autographs and even some pictures. There were a bunch of chairs set up in front of the Yankees dugout and a bunch of people with cameras and wires ran every which way. There were chairs for me, Emma, Scott, and Anthony, and a special chair at the end for Helen Winifred. I was sitting in the chair closest to Helen. I was actually pretty excited to talk with her. The last time I was on her show I was really nervous. This time I was feeling fine. After all, I was on the field at Yankee Stadium; what could be better?

"Keith, we are going to need you to switch chairs with Emma," a woman wearing a headset announced.

I switched seats, and then it hit me, I wasn't the star of the show anymore. Emma was. And she was about to have her moment in the spotlight. Not only was I really surprised by how okay I was with her taking over the company, but I was about to be on national TV, and I was actually relaxed!

Helen was still in the dugout talking with a bunch of players and a few reporters. When she finished up, she jogged over to where we were waiting.

"Hi, guys!" she said. "I am so happy to be meeting with you again. I love doing the shows here before the game!"

Some lady started putting makeup on my face.

"What are you doing?" I asked.

"I am putting makeup on you for the lights."

Anthony was laughing like crazy. "You can tell him the truth. You're a girl, Keith. I think you've always known it deep down."

"Whatever, Anthony! You are the one wearing a dress to the Yankees game."

"Come on, guys," Emma insisted. "No arguing in this Emmpire! Got it?"

"Emmpire?" Anthony asked.

"I'm in charge now, and I am calling this my Emmpire. Empire with two *m*'s like my name. And there is no arguing allowed, Anthony."

Anthony and I couldn't help but laugh. That was pretty clever for a five-year-old.

"I like your moxie," Helen told Emma.

My little sister might be exactly what we needed the whole time. Maybe now the two of us would find a way to get along better since we wouldn't be competing for top dog.

CHAPTER 31

Fart Me Out to the Ball Game

"Okay, everyone, we're going live in a few seconds. I hear you guys have been very busy since I saw you last," Helen said.

Before we could answer, a camera person yelled, "ACTION."

Helen turned to the camera. "I'm here today with the members of the youngest group of scientists I know. The last time I had them on the show it was a really wild time. Keith, who invented Sweet Farts, was trying to follow up his great experiment with something new. His goal was to discover a way to make foods that children hate to eat taste like foods children love. For example, he tried to make liver taste like candy canes. How's that going, Keith?"

"Well, I'm still working on the project and trying to get it just right. I promised my sister I would figure it out, and I will one of these days."

"Great! Anthony, how are you?"

"Awesome, Helen," Anthony said.

"Why the sarong, dude?" Helen asked. "Not that it doesn't look great on you with your Yankee jersey and all."

"Well, I traveled a bunch after my last time on the show, and I started wearing these on my trip. They're very comfortable," Anthony answered.

"Okay, so the last time you were here, you were in the audience, and you got an e-mail in the middle of the show and went totally crazy. Can you explain to everyone what happened that day?"

"Sure. I had been working on a pattern I found in the lottery numbers. I got the e-mail during your show telling me that I had won." Anthony looked about as happy as could be. He loved talking about his project and was eating this up. He was going on and on about his winnings, his tutor, and his trip around the world. It was a little hard to take. He didn't mention that he failed to come up with an idea for the AWSC.

"And that brings me to Emma, the new queen of the castle. I hear you are now in charge, young lady," Helen said.

"Yep, Mr. Gonzalez says I'm some kind of genius," she said.

"I love it! How has it been running the company?"

"I haven't been in charge that long. But now that I am, I want everyone in the company to start being nice and telling the truth." She turned to Anthony and me.

"Why? Who isn't telling the truth?" Helen asked.

"I just want everyone to know that Anthony has been blaming my brother Keith for his farts, and I think it's terrible. Haven't you, Anthony?"

I couldn't believe it! My little sister was calling Anthony out on national TV.

"No I haven't," Anthony started.

"Actually, you have," Emma said, turning back to Helen. "You see, Helen, Anthony is a flatulist. He can fart whenever he wants. He's been farting all over the place for as long as I can remember and blaming Keith all along."

I was in shock, Scott was in shock, and Anthony was definitely in shock.

Helen looked a little confused. "Okay, this is going in a direction I hadn't expected. Is this true, Keith?" she asked.

Anthony suddenly looked really embarrassed. I sort of felt bad for him, in fact. I don't like seeing anyone feel bad. But he did have this coming.

"All I can say, Helen, is what I've been saying for years. Anthony was the one farting at school. No one ever believed me. I'm glad Emma does."

"Well, Anthony?" Helen asked. "Is there anything you want to say to us?"

Anthony sat quietly for a few seconds as we all waited for his answer. Then he just stood up and ran into the dugout and down the clubhouse steps.

Helen looked even more confused. "Well, *I* can honestly say that it is never boring when I have you kids on the show."

"You should hang around the lab. That's nothing," Emma added. Helen continued with her interview, asking Emma more about her experiment. They talked about all the work Emma had done and how she found that animals help cheer people up, and when people are happy, they tend to be healthier. Helen loved Emma's project. She even talked about her own animals. The two of them were really hitting it off.

Scott nudged me in the side. I ignored him, keeping my attention on Emma and Helen. He nudged me again and whispered, "When am I going to get to talk?" He must have been going crazy. He was so worried that Mr. Gonzalez was unhappy with his work, and here was his chance to show off his new experiment. I shrugged. It seemed like Emma and Helen might talk forever. It was fun to see Emma in the spotlight and having such a good time with it, though.

Then I heard a sound that my ears couldn't quite grasp. It was the loudest and strangest farting noise I'd ever heard, and it was coming out of the speakers all around the stadium. It wasn't just a fart. It was a song. It was a song being farted!

I looked up at the huge TV screens and there was Anthony. He was farting "Take Me Out to the Ball Game." Everyone in the stadium stopped what they were doing and looked up at the screens. The players, the hotdog guys, the ushers, the fans, EVERYBODY!

Helen spoke first. "I'm not exactly sure what I'm seeing."

"I told you," Emma said giggling. "He's a flatulist."

"That is the most disgusting thing I've ever witnessed!" Helen concluded. "I think we better go to commercial." But the cameraman kept filming, giving her a thumbs-up as he continued to record Anthony's baseball tribute.

When the whole thing was over, Anthony shouted, "I'm Anthony Papas! Otherwise known as Sir Anthony the Farter, and I'm a flatulist. I'm sorry I tortured you all these years, Keith. Now PLAY BALL!" The crowd went crazy cheering for Anthony. It was just like him. I had been embarrassed about farts all these years, and here he was farting on the big screen at Yankee Stadium and getting a standing ovation to boot.

Sweet Farts

CHAPTER 32

All Hail the Queen

After we finished up with Helen, we got to stay for the game. It was amazing. We had awesome seats, and the Yankees won in the ninth with a walk-off homerun.

In the limousine on the way home, I was feeling pretty good. "Anthony, I can't believe that you finally admitted to the world that you are a farter."

"Yeah, I know. You've said that to me about ten times already. I still can't believe Emma did that to me on TV. I'm sorry I did all those crazy things to you."

Anthony had a way of surprising me sometimes. As cruel and strange as he was most of the time, there were times when he was just a regular kid.

"It's okay. I'm just happy I won't be S.B.D. or Farts Emerson or Goozer anymore at school."

"Oh, I'm pretty sure those nicknames are going to stick to you like glue. Besides, I don't plan to stop calling you those names anytime soon."

"Thanks, but I think that once people know it was you all along, you may get a few nicknames yourself."

"I know. That's why I gave myself the nickname Sir Anthony the Farter before other kids could think of a name for me."

"When are you going to learn to get along already?" Emma interrupted.

"We *are* kind of getting along right now, Emma," I said.

"I agree, Emma," Mr. Gonzalez added. "You two must learn to treat each other better. Learn to work together, not against one another. In case you haven't noticed, while you two were busy arguing and trying to get all the power these past few weeks, you were outsmarted by a five-year-old."

"I still can't believe that Emma was working on science when we thought she was just playing with animals," Scott said.

"You guys thought she was just playing because none of you took the time to ask her what she was doing," Mr. Gonzalez said.

"It looked like she was playing because she seemed to be having so much fun," Anthony said.

"That's the part of this that you guys need to learn. The reason Emma made it look so easy is because she *was* having fun. She thought of something she already enjoyed, and she experimented around that."

"Maybe you guys can do an experiment on arguing," Emma suggested with a laugh. "And since none of you came up with the new scents for Sweet Farts that Mr. Stuart wanted, I have decided. The four new scents for Sweet Farts this summer will be *Salami, Pastrami, Pickle Deluxe,* and *Blue Octopus*," she announced.

"Emma, those scents don't even make sense. And *Blue Octopus* isn't even a smell," I said.

"I like those scents. I think they're funny and people like funny things."

"The first three scents are okay, Emma, but I don't understand *Blue Octopus*," Mr. Gonzalez replied.

"*Blue Octopus* is my favorite," she said. "I think it will be your favorite, too, Anthony."

"Why is that?" Anthony asked.

"Because *Blue Octopus* won't change the scent of gas at all, so it will be DEADLY!"

Mr. Gonzalez smiled. "Clever, Emm, very clever. *Blue Octopus* it is."

I had to hand it to her, it was pretty good.

"So whoever has the best idea for the next fair will be in charge, right?" Anthony asked.

Mr. Gonzalez laughed. "No, Anthony, Emma is in charge of Sweet Farts and will continue to be as long as she shows she can handle it. We said the winner of the challenge would run the company. Remember when I warned you about being careful what you wish for, you just might get it? In this case, you boys got exactly what you wished for."

"Welcome to the Emmpire. I am your queen," Emma said, raising her hands in the air in a victory salute.

Mr. Gonzalez was right. We had wished for the smartest person to lead the company going forward, and we had gotten exactly what we wished for. I just never dreamed that the smartest person in the company would be my little sister. She was the queen of the Emmpire. I was blown away.

About the Author

Raymond Bean is the Amazon best-selling author of the Sweet Farts series. Writing for kids who claim they don't like reading, his books have ranked #1 in children's humor, humorous series, and fantasy and adventure genres, and the Sweet Farts series is consistently in Amazon's top 100 books for children. His second book, *Sweet Farts #2: Rippin' It Old School*, was Amazon Publishing's very first children's release. Foreign editions of his books have been released in Germany and Korea, and editions for Italy, Brazil, and Turkey are forthcoming.